HEIRESS OF EMBERS

KINGDOM OF FAIRYTALES BOOK 2

J. A. ARMITAGE

"Touch it, my dear. Touch the spindle. No need to worry." The beautiful young woman with startling black eyes that shone like dark diamonds with flashes of green urged. And the spindle itself. I'd never seen a piece of machinery so wonderful, so intriguing. So forbidden. It was only a contraption made to spin wool. Not harmful. But it was so tempting. I'd always been the good girl, kept to the straight and narrow, but this was something else. The woman had promised me nothing, and yet, she made me feel that this would be the answer to all my prayers if I only did the unthinkable.

I reached out, my forefinger extended, every fiber of my being, wanting...no, needing to touch it. The one thing I'd learned my whole life never to touch. Glancing back to the woman, she nodded her head, a smile on her face. A face with high cheekbones and a severity that came with the beauty she had. She mesmerized me with her strange horned headpiece and clear delight. I wanted to please her almost as much as I wanted to touch the spindle for myself.

A glint of light hit the needle, enticing me further. It was just so beautiful...so perfect.

"Do it! Do it, Azia."

I reached forward and touched the needle. A sharp pain shot through my finger, and I screamed out. Everything went black...

"Ouch!" My eyes shot open as I banged my head on my headboard. My breathing came raggedly as I took in my surroundings. I was in my room. Everything looked normal except for the bump appearing on my head. It was a dream. I'd dreamed about her, the witch that had cursed my mother. I wondered if my mother had been so taken by her when she fell into the spell. It had felt so real.

I didn't want to believe the doctor that my mother's sleep was a curse any more than my father did, but the fact remained that every doctor my father had brought in to see her had agreed that apart from the fact she was asleep, there was nothing wrong with her. None of them used the word curse, but they didn't need to. This happened to her the first time after she pricked her finger on a spindle. She couldn't have done that this time. Spindles didn't exist in Draconis anymore. They were illegal. Except...except I'd seen one just days before in a shop in Zhore. I'd bought my mittens in the shop. The shopkeeper had been urging me to touch the needle on that one too. Why hadn't I thought of it before? The shock of my dream brought back the memory with startling clarity, except the woman had looked different. I thought back to the woman I'd seen in the shop. She was older than the woman from my dream. My chest tightened as I wondered if I could have stopped all this by telling my father earlier. Jumping out of bed, I pulled my nightgown around me and tripped over my slippers in my rush to see him. Maybe I should have told him earlier, but I couldn't turn back time. I could only tell him what I knew now and hope he wasn't too angry with me.

I rushed out of my bedroom, smack bang into Milo.

"Where are you going in such a rush?"

His hand brushed my arm, and worry showed in his beautiful brown eyes. Jack eyed us curiously from the end of the corridor, causing me to speak in a hushed tone.

"I remembered something I saw last week that might help my mother," I said, pulling him away from Jack. "I don't know why I didn't think of it yesterday when all those doctors were going in and out."

Milo pulled me close to him. I guess he didn't care what Jack thought of us. "I'm so sorry about your mother, Azia. I wanted to come to you last night, but I knew you were with your parents, and then I thought you'd need your sleep."

I nodded. "I wish you had come to my room too. I barely slept, anyway."

It was an invitation. Who cared if Jack overheard. It didn't matter anymore. My mother was asleep in a curse, and my father was beside himself with stress. My life was falling apart, and nobody cared if I was going to get married or not.

He pulled me into a hug, holding me tightly, keeping out the world. It was all too brief.

I kissed him quickly and left him to work. The not having a boyfriend/fake boyfriend/not-so-fake boyfriend was not going well, or it was going too well. Who knew? The whole thing was complicated, but I knew that having Milo around was what I needed right now. The consequences of our new relationship were not something I had the brainpower to worry about at the moment. I found my father where I'd left him the night before, sitting in an armchair beside his own bed. He looked up as I closed the door behind me. His eyes were red as though he'd been crying, and the dark circles that had plagued my mother in her final days awake now rested under my father's eyes.

"I didn't want to disturb her," he said, by way of explanation, though it explained nothing at all. A horse could ride across the bed, and she wouldn't wake up. Still, my father was in pieces. He needed help, not logic.

"Why don't you have a shower and nap in one of the guest rooms for a while? I will stay with her until you come back."

He nodded slowly, pulling himself out of the chair. His clothes were the same clothes he'd been wearing the previous day. He'd not even taken off his boots. The bottom of his untucked shirt rested over the line of his belt, and one button had come open. After kissing my mother, he ambled past me, giving me a pat on the shoulder as he passed. I'd never seen him look so defeated.

My mother lay in peaceful slumber. Once again, she was Sleeping Beauty. I could well imagine how my father had fallen in love with her all those years ago, just by looking at her. I didn't believe in love at first sight. That was the stuff of romance books and fairy tales, but I could see why my parents were attracted to each other. They grew as a couple from there. I Sighed. Going to sleep and waking up with my soul mate would be so much easier than falling for my fake boyfriend and then having to marry someone I detested.

The only good thing about my mother being cursed was the fact that the fae had kept a low profile. I knew he was in the castle somewhere, but I'd not seen him since the curse took over. Of all the people in the castle, he would be the best one to speak to about the curse. He was the only person of magic in the castle. Correction. He was the only person of magic in the whole castle apart from me, but seeing as I only just found out I was magic, I was no use when it came to curses.

I tried to conjure up some magic over my mother's body,

but nothing came of it. I felt too dull and depressed to muster up the energy needed, and I didn't want to explode her like I did with an apple only a few days before.

I sat with my mother only twenty minutes before my father returned. He'd changed clothes and showered, at least, but the pallor on his skin and the deathly tired look in his eyes remained.

I stood up to let him sit back down.

"I couldn't sleep," he mumbled, sitting back into his chair and resting his head in his hands. "How can I sleep knowing that your mother is deep in a curse? I don't know what to do, Azia. Last time kissing her was all I needed to do, but now when I try...nothing. Her eyelids don't even flicker."

I took a deep breath and psyched myself up for my confession. Now was the time to tell him what I'd seen the other day.

"When we were in Zhore, I went into a wool shop to buy mittens. In the window was a spindle. I didn't tell you sooner because I thought it was just for show. I didn't expect anything like this to happen. I'm sorry, Father."

My father licked his dry lips and sighed. "I don't think your mother visited Zhore yesterday, so I doubt that has anything to do with the curse, but I'll get someone to look. Thank you for letting me know."

"The woman behind the counter was strange," I added. "She wanted me to touch the needle. It felt like I was being compelled to do it. I would have, too, if you'd not walked in the shop."

My father's eyebrows furrowed. "It is a strange coincidence. I'll speak to the castle guards and ask if anyone saw your mother leaving yesterday. If there is a spindle there, it needs to be destroyed, even if it is harmless."

I jumped at the chance of leaving the castle. "Let me go. I know where the shop is."

He moved closer to the bed and gazed upon my mother. "There are things you do not know and things I promised her I'd never tell you. I do not wish to revisit the past, and yet it seems the past is revisiting me. I cannot let you go. I'm sorry. I remember the shop you spoke about though I don't recall seeing the spindle. My guards will find it."

I remembered how real it had all felt. How much I needed to touch the spindle. My dream. "Do you think the curse was meant for me, Father?"

My father took my mother's hand and looked my way. "I do not know, Azia. We are powerful people, and with power comes enemies. It is possible that someone out there wanted to recreate what happened to your mother all those years ago. You need Caspian keeping you safe now more than ever."

I resisted the urge to roll my eyes at the mention of the fae. "Don't you think it could be the same person who cursed mother before?"

"No," he said, standing up abruptly. "That woman is long gone. It is impossible."

"That woman? Who?" I knew whom he was referring to. I just wanted him to acknowledge it.

"I do not wish to talk about it," he said, striding over to me. "And I do not wish to talk about her."

I sucked in a breath, heart hammering at the name on my lips. "Is it Derillen?"

He looked me dead in the eyes. "I do not know where you learned that name. We never mentioned her to the press, but it doesn't matter. She is dead. She has to be. I do not wish to discuss the matter further."

"Ok, Father," I said quietly, nodding my head. "I'll find a guard and let him know where the wool shop is"

He nodded. "Thank you....and, Azia?"

"Yes?"

"I do not think this is your fault, and I do not want you thinking it is. I would have thought nothing of a spindle either."

I left him there, my mind swirling with everything he'd told me. Long ago, I'd thought my parents had been honest with me about my birth and adoption, and because I was happy, I'd never thought to question it. I was very young when they told me I was adopted, and they'd always assured me that, adopted or not, I was still the heir to the Draconis throne and just as important to them as Remy, Ash, and Hollis. By rights, the throne should have gone to Remy as the real blood-born son of the king and queen, but my parents had decided to treat me as they would as if I was born to them. I wanted to believe I wasn't part of this, but the weird compulsion to touch the spindle had been playing with my thoughts. Whatever my father said, I knew that this was something to do with me, and my mother had somehow gotten caught in the crossfire. I needed to find out who I was and where I'd come from, and my father would not tell me. It was also certain that I would go against my father's wishes. I'd never done it before, but there was no way I would mope around the castle like him. The problem of the dragons was nowhere nearer to being solved, no one knew what was wrong with my mother, and now we had a spindle to destroy. At the moment, my father was not capable of dealing with any of it, which left it to me. And I knew which guard to ask to come with me...

"Your father asked for me to come into Zhore with you?" Milo cocked an eyebrow.

"Not exactly," I hedged. "I made an executive decision, but seeing as he's in with my mother and everyone is too scared to bother him over trivialities, I figured it may as well be you as anyone else."

"Great!" he said, his eyes shining.

"I have a job for Milo," I shouted over to Jack, who watched us with curiosity. He frowned, knowing he'd be guarding the corridor alone, but there was nothing he could say or do about it.

As soon as we were in the stables and away from the prying eyes of the castle staff, I took Milo's hand in mine. Illicit, and yet it felt so right. My engagement with the fae had still not happened and hopefully never would. Maybe when this mess was all over, we could go back to how everything used to be, and I could decide whether or not I wanted a boyfriend.

"Don't you think it's weird?" Milo asked as he heaved himself up upon one of the castle horses.

"What?"

He waited until I'd mounted my horse to continue. "So many things going on at once. I've heard the phrase 'I've not seen anything like this in eighteen years' so many times this past week, mostly from Jack, but I've heard it from others too. The townsfolk are gossiping, and it isn't good. They say that things are going back to how they used to be, and it scares them. I'm sorry to say this, Azia, but they need a leader, and your father isn't up to the job at the moment. Not that I'd expect him to be in his situation, but..."

I sighed as we headed out into the cold. He was right. I'd been so caught up in everything going on in the castle that I'd not thought about the townspeople or the state of the kingdom. It stood to reason that everyone was scared. Giant dragons were invading every other day, and the queen was back under her curse. I hurried a glance up into the sky, but clouds obscured the peak of the mountains, and I couldn't see the dragons.

"I've been thinking of the flip side to that," I said, trotting along the path that would lead us to Zhore. "Everyone is talking about things going back to how they used to be, but no one has mentioned why things changed for the better all those years ago. One minute everything was horrible, and then overnight, everything became rosy."

Milo pulled to the side of the road to skirt around a muddy patch where the snow had thawed. "You know, I'd not thought about it like that before, but you are right. The change back then must have been as startling as it is now. Your father broke your mother's curse. Maybe that had something to do with it."

"He did," I said, following him around the muddy patch, "but he told me that the curse was already weakening. He was able to get through the brambles much easier than anyone else. Why? My father was no one special before then."

"He was your mother's true love," Milo pointed out.

I rolled my eyes. "Oh, please! He'd never even met her before that day. He only knew of her beauty through legends. No one was alive that remembered her. And have you seen my mother? Every man who meets her falls in love with her instantly. At best, he kissed her without permission. It was practically abuse."

Milo laughed as I caught back up to him. "Your parent's story is the most romantic story ever told, and you've turned it into a felony. I think it's sweet. Maybe they really were made for each other, and it was love at first sight. Have you thought of that?"

"Love at first sight is a fallacy," I huffed. "It doesn't exist."

"Doesn't it?" He turned his brown eyes to me and gave me a meaningful look that made my stomach flutter.

Zhore town square looked so much different from the last time I'd seen it. The decorations from New Year's Eve had long been cleared away, and now it was perfectly clean. Clean and empty with a light dusting of snow. In a marked difference to a few days ago when my father had given a speech, there wasn't a soul to be seen. The shops were all closed, many of them shuttered up.

"What's going on?" I asked nervously.

"I told you people are scared. No one dares open their shops. No one dares go outside. Those that aren't frightened of the dragons are scared of the curse. Last time the whole castle was cursed, but people wonder if this time it will hit the town too, or even the whole kingdom. Everywhere is closed but the Dragon Roost Inn. It's making a roaring trade. People are drinking to forget."

I swallowed back a small laugh. At least someone was having some good luck amidst all of this.

I walked the horse over to the dark alley at the back of the square and dismounted. The shop with the spindle was still there, and in the window, the spindle stood where it had before.

"This is it," I exclaimed, my pulse running faster at the sight of it.

Dismounting, I tied the horse up and wandered over to the window. As I had felt before, a strange feeling came over me. This time I recognized it for what it was. Magic. Cautiously I beckoned Milo over.

"Do you feel that?" I asked.

Milo glanced around him as though this feeling would suddenly materialize out of thin air.

He shrugged his shoulders. "Feel what?"

Maybe I could only feel it because I was magic too. Maybe it didn't affect him the same way it had me, but it was there. Its suffocating presence squeezed at me, wrapping itself around me like a blanket of invisible fog.

"Never mind," I said, taking his hand. "Let's get that spindle."

"Go in?" he looked at me with a puzzled expression. "It's empty. I can see from here that there is nothing in there.

They probably packed up and moved at the first sign of trouble. You can't blame them. I mean, who would be stupid enough to put a spindle in a shop window? Especially in this climate."

My eyes widened. "Are you being serious? The spindle is right there." I pointed through the shop window even though we were but inches away from it.

He let go of my hand and moved towards the window, placing his face right up to the glass, the way a child might gaze into a sweet shop.

"It's empty, Azia. It looks like there's not been anyone here for a while."

He was staring right at the spindle, and he couldn't see it. I wondered if my father had seen it when he'd come looking for me the other day or if he'd only seen me in an empty shop.

A thrill of fear shot through me as I took in the repercussions of what I was seeing. If Milo couldn't see it and I could, it meant one thing. That the spindle was there for me. My theory that this had more to do with me than my mother intensified.

I hesitantly pushed on the shop door, and it opened easily. The shop looked as it had before with wool and woolen items filling the shelves. The buzz of magical energy intensified as I walked through the door.

"Let's go. Milo said, taking my hand again. This place gives me the creeps."

Just then, a woman appeared behind the counter. It was the same woman I'd seen before, but this time, she couldn't be more different. Her shawl had transformed into a cape, the hat on her head shaped into two horns. This is how she had appeared in my dreams. Younger, more fearsome. Panic gripped me as she pointed her finger.

"You," she shrieked. "You did this! This is all your fault."

A ball of green magic appeared in her hand, swirling hypnotically. She leveled it at Milo and threw, hitting him square in the chest. As it hit him, he turned to stone. Unmoving, unblinking.

"Milo!" I screamed, but he didn't answer...couldn't answer.

"What have you done?" I screeched.

She cackled and pulled on her energy again. Feeling for my own magic, I tried to recreate the same as I'd done out on the moor with Caspian, but it wouldn't come. In the grips of fear, I couldn't pull my energy inside, so I did the next best thing. Pulling my sword from my side, I charged her. There was no fear in her eyes, only amusement, but as the sword pushed deep into her belly, her eyes opened wide.

"Mark my words, I will get you," she hissed and then turned unto purple and green smoke, evaporating in the air. The shop around me fell away until all there was left were empty shelves and cobwebs that looked like they had been there for years.

"This place needs a good clean is what it needs."

I turned to find Milo looking as good as new, wiping dust from a shelf. He'd not even noticed he had been petrified. Behind him, the storefront was empty. The spindle was no longer there.

"Did you see that?" I choked out, but I already knew his answer.

"See what?"

His eyes roamed the empty shop, searching for something that he couldn't see.

I took Milo's hand, thankful that it was warm and real. He hadn't seen the magic, but I sure had. Whoever this woman was, she was connected to my mother's curse, and not only that, she now wanted me.

"Come on, let's go."

Milo studied me through curious eyes. "Where?"

"We are heading back to the castle," I replied, dragging him from the shop. "There's someone I need to see."

I FOUND Caspian in the drawing room, a bag by his side. He was dressed in a powder blue waistcoat with gold trim and a gold fob watch on a chain leading to his pocket.

"Are you leaving?" I asked, though it was obvious he was.

"Yes," he muttered. "I've booked tickets on the Urbis Express from Zhore for this afternoon. You've made it very clear that I'm not wanted, and as your mother is sick, I feel that my time here is done. You have your wish granted, Azia."

I hated the next words I would speak, but I spoke them anyway. "Please stay. I need your help."

He tutted and waved his hand as though I no longer mattered. "I see. Now that you need me, you want me to stay. I'm nobody's pawn, not even yours, princess."

My stomach churned. He was right, and I could hardly deny it, but I needed him. He was the only connection I had to a magic world, a world in which the evil woman from the wool shop had tried to hurt me. I sat next to him on the sofa.

"I met a woman today..."

"How delightful," he growled.

"She was a witch," I replied, ignoring his sarcasm. "I think she was the same witch that put my mother in a curse, and I think she was the same witch that did it the first time. I think it was Derillen."

He sat toward me, his lips bared. "If it was Derillen, you wouldn't be here to tell the tale."

I matched his pose, leaning in toward him. I wasn't about to be threatened by him. "I saw her, and I did survive. She was tall and thin with a cap of horns."

I saw a momentary flicker of fear in his eyes. "It's not possible. She is dead."

"Why would she have an interest in me?"

He stood and picked up his bag. "I've said too much. None of this is my business. I tried helping your father eighteen years ago, and I've tried helping him now, but I can plainly see that my use here extends only to being a fount of knowledge to you. I've already told you to speak to your parents, now good day, I have an airship to catch."

He made to walk, but the door to the drawing room opened before he could reach it. My father walked in. When he saw Caspian, his expression turned into one of surprise.

"Where are you heading, my friend?"

Caspian turned and indicated me. "Your daughter has made it perfectly clear that I am unwanted here. I'm heading back to The Forge. At least there, people have manners... Well, some of them have."

My father cast a warning glance over Caspian's shoulder, directed at me. He then turned his attention back to his friend. "Caspian, you are more than welcome to stay here in the castle, despite what my daughter thinks. I wouldn't hear of you leaving us."

Caspian held up his hand. "Your offer is kind, but I see no reason to stay. I've already told you, I cannot break the curse on Briar Rose, and as marriage to your daughter is no longer on the table, my time here is done. Farewell."

"Nonsense." My father clapped him on the shoulder and led him back to the sofa. "Who said anything about marriage being off the table? I know that Briar Rose was having the staff here look after you, but I believe they will continue to do so in her...absence. We planned for you to marry Azia, and you will." He paused for a minute, his finger up to his lips, deep in thought. "The wedding will happen three weeks from today. I'll get my staff to prepare. I'll tell Briar Rose. If there is anything she will wake up for, it is our daughter's wedding."

A surge of nausea took my breath away. "But Father..."

"But Father nothing," he began, his tone changing to one of anger. "You've disobeyed me more than once this week. I know you went to Zhore, despite me forbidding it, and I know you went with that Milo chap. I've got enough on my plate without having to worry about a wayward daughter. Your mother wanted you to marry Caspian, and so do I. I never wanted to force you into marriage, Azia, but with your wilful ways, you've forced my hand. The wedding will go ahead. I suggest you spend the next three weeks getting to know Caspian because you'll soon be living with him."

"But..."

"Don't," he warned, leveling a finger at me. "I am the king, and the last time I checked, you are my daughter. You will do as I say."

I lowered my head in submission. "Yes, sir."

"Good."

My stomach churned, but anger at my father shouldn't stop me from telling him what I saw. My mother's life was at stake.

"I saw a woman today," I said. "She had a spindle. I saw her use magic. She turned Milo to stone, but when I stabbed her with my sword, the spell on Milo was broken."

The anger in my father fell away and was replaced with concern. "What did she look like?"

"Alec," Caspian cautioned.

I took a deep breath as I recalled the woman and how she looked now. "She was tall with horns and angular cheekbones."

My father turned on the spot, running his hands through his hair. "No."

"Your daughter could have been imagining it, Your Highness," Caspian said, narrowing his eyes at me.

"I wasn't imagining anything," I persisted. "She turned to smoke when I stabbed her."

My father stormed out of the door. I followed quickly, Caspian behind me.

"You," my father barked at one of the guards. "Round up all my men. All the Draconis Army. I want every single man out looking for spindles. Scour the whole kingdom. I will not rest until every last one is in the courtyard and on a bonfire. " He turned to me. "Azia, you can go to your room. I don't want you coming out until I say so."

He stormed off up the stairs as the guard ran outside to alert the other guards.

"What's happening?" I asked, fear gripping me. "Is the witch that cursed my mother back?"

Caspian drew me into a hug that was strong and surprisingly tender for such a jackass. He stroked my hair. "Let's hope for all our sakes she's not, princess, because last time no one could defeat her. No one at all."

I sat on my bed, gazing out of the window, sorrow filling my soul. Exhaustion crippled me, but sleep had only happened in fits and starts, and every time I closed my eyes, I saw her face. The witch, with her heavily contoured face and cheekbones like knives. Why had my magic not worked?

I patted the sword on the bed next to me, running my fingers over the beautifully shaped metalwork. It, too, was magic, but the magic it possessed wasn't mine. It belonged to the dwarves. It had been them that had turned the witch to smoke, not anything I had done. I was surprised that I was still allowed to keep it. I'd even briefly mentioned it to my father the night before, but he'd not said anything, and so, I'd brought it back to my room and slept with it by my side.

A small knock on the door took my concentration away, and a quick look at the clock told me it was only a little after four am. I guess I wasn't the only one who couldn't sleep.

"Who is it?" I asked quietly.

"It's me."

I leapt out of bed, knocking my sword to the floor with a

clatter. Opening the door, I pulled Milo inside and brought him into a kiss. I'd hoped he would come to my room last night. If I was going to be honest with myself, that was part of the reason I hadn't slept. I was betrothed to one man, but my heart now belonged to another. My father had ordered me to marry Caspian, and after the wedding, I would be the dutiful daughter and wife and be true to him. I owed it to my parents. They had taken me in as a newborn and made me a princess. The heir to the Draconis throne. They had given me a wonderful childhood and everything I could ever dream about. In exchange, I would do as they wanted. Up until then, though, I was nobody's but my own.

Milo kissed me back, his lips crushing against mine, matching the urgency. This kiss had to say it all because I would break down if I had to say it in words.

Milo's arms held me, pulling me into him, our bodies fitting together like puzzle pieces. My hand ran through his hair as I held onto him, fearful of letting go in case this was our last kiss.

He lay me down on the bed, his body on mine. An unwanted image of when Caspian had done the same thing flittered through my mind. Except he'd been pinning me down with a sword to my throat.

"I'm engaged," I whispered, blinking back the tears.

Milo pulled back until I could no longer feel the weight of him on me. I sat up to find him hunched over on the bed.

"I didn't expect you to say that after pulling me into your room and kissing me like that," he sighed.

"I don't want to be."

He looked up and took my hand in his. "I know you don't, but it's probably for the best anyway."

I furrowed my eyebrows. "What do you mean?"

"Your father has ordered all his men out to look for spindles," Milo explained.

I already knew that, but it never occurred to me that Milo would be one of the men to go.

"You're leaving?" I asked. I had so little time with him until my wedding that I couldn't bear him going away for any of it. I needed him.

He nodded. "That's what I came up to tell you. I've been assigned to one of the towns, but I won't know which one until I leave. I was going to ask if I can be kept in Zhore so I could still see you, but I guess it's best if they send me somewhere far away if you are marrying Caspian."

My heart bottomed out. "I don't want you to go." What had I done? Now not only was I going to be marrying the fae, I was also going to lose Milo for the three weeks I had left. "It's not fair."

Milo shook his head "No, it's not, but life never is fair. We get what we get, and it's how we deal with it that counts. "

"I planned to spend the next three weeks with you," I explained. "I had it planned out. We were going to go into the woods and practice sword fighting every day and..."—my voice choked up—"I planned lots of kissing."

"Is that when you are getting married? In three weeks?" The look on his face damn near broke my heart.

I nodded slowly.

"Then, it is right that I leave," he said brusquely, standing up from the bed. "You will be safe. Jack is staying here to guard the corridor. He's been told not to let you out of your room. I thought it was because of everything going on, but now, I see it's so you don't sneak out to see me."

He walked to the door. I ran after him, catching his arm.

"There is a chance I won't have to marry him," I whispered as he spun to face me. "Remy found a chapter in an old book about a competition for the princess's hand in marriage."

"I remember. You told me before, but I think it is too late

for that. I'd hoped that it would never come to that, and now, I don't think it will. I would have fought for you, Azia. I would have fought with everything that I had, but I'm not sure you want to fight anymore. Maybe The fae will give you everything you need."

He closed the door behind him, and I broke down. Tears cascaded down my face as I flung myself onto the bed.

He was wrong. I wanted to fight. I wanted Milo, but how could I go against my father's wishes when the whole kingdom was falling apart?

Another knock on my door had me stumbling out of bed again. I wiped my tears on the back of my sleeve in a very un-princess-like manner and opened the door. My heart fell as I found Jack there instead of Milo.

He held out a flower. "Milo asked me to give you this," he growled. "I don't like it, mind you. I don't like it one bit, and it's good that he's gone. I told him it would lead to no good, you being a princess and him being a guard, but would he listen? Youth today!"

I took the flower from his hand. It was a poppy. No poppies grew around here and certainly not in the winter, but he'd found it anyway. Maybe he'd bought it from one of the expensive flower shops in Zhore. They imported flowers from other kingdoms. This one probably came all the way from Floris, the kingdom famous for its flowers. I thanked Jack and closed the door, my heart in pieces.

Two hours later, I had another knock on the door. This time the door opened without me answering, and Dahlia bustled in.

"Are you still in bed?" she asked. "Lazy girl, come on. Let's get you bathed."

"I don't want to bathe," I huffed, but Dahlia ignored me as she so often did, and from the small bathroom, I heard the taps being turned on.

"Heartbreak doesn't give you an excuse for being dirty young miss," she admonished, coming out of the bathroom with a towel and throwing it at me.

"Who said anything about me being heartbroken?" I picked up the white towel and sat up.

"No one, but I'm not blind. I might be old, but these eyes are as good as yours. I've seen you sneaking out with that young guard of yours, and this morning, I saw all the guards being sent off to look for spindles. I also heard on the grapevine that your wedding to that charming Mr. Caspian is being planned."

"You know about that?"

"Know about it?" she exclaimed. "I'm the head of the planning committee."

I sighed, falling back on the bed. "I don't want to marry him, Dahlia. I don't love him. I don't even like the guy. He's a creep."

"That's as may be," she said, pulling me out of bed so she could straighten the sheets, "But he's very handsome. Very, very handsome. You are a lucky girl."

I rolled my eyes. "Hmph. He's an idiot, and he's nearly as old as my father."

"I'd wager he's a lot older than that," she said as she fussed with my pillowcase. "Fae age differently than we human folk do. He doesn't look it, though. He'd pass for being in his early twenties with that fine physique of his... and oh, that hair!"

Her eyes misted over as she spoke.

"Dahlia!" I snapped.

"Sorry. I got carried away with myself. I have to say you are wrong about one thing, though. That man is no idiot. He's a smart cookie. I saw him with a suitcase yesterday. He said he was leaving to head back to The Forge. He said he had a ticket booked on the Urbis Express and everything."

"Yes, so?"

She ushered me into the bathroom and turned off the taps.

"That suitcase. I picked it up to take it back to his room for him, and I'm telling you now, it was as light as a feather."

"What do you mean?" I asked, though I had a suspicion I already knew.

"I mean, it was empty. He'd not packed at all. He had no intention of going back to The Forge."

"Why the stinking...rotten...double crossing..."

Dahlia laughed as she pulled my nightdress over my head. "He'll keep you on your toes will that one, and that's half a marriage right there. You want someone who will excite you. Life will never be boring with that one around."

I splashed down into the bath, letting water drip all over the sides. I was going to kill him. Excitement? I would slice his head off way before I got to my honeymoon night. I wanted to please my father; I really did, but if I was going to survive my first week of marriage to that creep, I would have to be in a different room from him. We would, quite literally, kill each other.

"You know..." I shouted back through the open door to my bedroom where Dahlia had gone to tidy up. "If I don't marry him, that means he's available. Maybe, he'd like a beautiful maid by his side?"

"Get away with ya! I'm an old woman. What would he do with the likes of me? He's got rich blood, that one. Oh, if wishes were pennies, we'd all be rich."

She drifted off into song, leaving me to soak and think of everything she'd said. Caspian really was good looking. Fantastic looking. Carved by the gods gorgeous, and yet, he drove me crazy.

I wasn't ready for marriage. All I'd ever seen of it was my mother and father, and they pranced around like newlyweds all the time. I couldn't see Caspian and I being like that.

Tempestuous was the best way I could think to describe a marriage with Caspian, and that was being nice. Bloody awful was the real term I was thinking of.

He didn't even want me. He wanted power. Maybe he wanted to overthrow my father. It wouldn't surprise me. He wasn't beyond lying and subterfuge to get what he wanted. I'd seen that for myself.

"Urgh," I said, which turned into a gurgle as I lowered my face into the water. If wishes were pennies...I'd be a mermaid like the people of Atlantice, and I'd never get out of this bath ever again. As it was, I wasn't a mermaid, and lying with my head under the water would drown me, so I had to come up for air eventually.

After my bath, I let Dahlia choose my clothes and dress me. I usually fought her every step of the way, preferring to choose my own clothes and dress myself, but this morning, I didn't care what I wore. What did it matter when I was nothing more than a prisoner in my own room? When she was done, I sat by the window as she brushed my hair— another job I hated having done for me.

Outside, hundreds of guards crowded around the court-yard. One of the men I recognized as Gerard, the man who trained the guards and was the highest in command of the army. He was shouting orders, getting everyone into groups. Next to him, stood Jacob, the man who'd argued with my father about the wall being erected around the Fire Mountains, a grim expression on his face and his arms folded across his chest. He didn't look any happier with the thought of going out to find spindles than he'd been about erecting a wall. He was the type of guy who wanted action, and in his case, that meant taking his men up the mountains and killing all the dragons. As I watched, another group set out on horseback. I looked for Milo, but I couldn't see him amongst all the other young men with helmets on. As the men set out, the number in the courtyard became smaller, and I was forced to realize that I'd already missed him. He'd already gone, and with him, my heart. It wasn't a dangerous mission, and yet, my nerves were on edge as though something bad was going to happen.

"You were around when my mother woke up the first time, right?" I asked Dahlia.

Dahlia had been my maid my whole life. She'd also been my governess when I was very young before my parents brought in tutors for my brothers and me. If anyone knew anything about Derillen, it was she.

"I wasn't one of the staff here at the palace that was cursed along with your mother," she replied. "They were all given a pension for life and told to leave and have fun. It was a generous settlement, by all accounts. They were given the option to stay if they desired, but none did. They'd all given enough service, and they had enough money to live the rest of their lives comfortably. Your grandfather was a very generous man. I was hired just after that. Your grandmother hired me."

My grandparents had died when I was young. I barely remembered my grandmother at all.

"She was a lovely lady," Dahlia continued. "Busy, though. She was in charge of filling the castle with staff again. Your grandfather might have been generous, but he wasn't very clever. He let all his staff go at once, and so, your grandmother spent weeks trying to find staff again. My first few weeks here were hectic. I was doing about eight people's jobs already when you came along."

My curiosity peaked. "What happened with that? Did my parents go to an adoption agency?"

She stopped tugging my hair for a second. "I don't know, lovey. I was cleaning the rooms one day when I was handed a baby. I don't know where you came from. I do remember how surprising it was. Your parents were still in that lovely honeymoon phase. They never left their room except for food."

I blushed at the thought of my parents on honeymoon. Their love was already barf-worthy.

She began tugging at my hair again, pulling through the knots. "I remember thinking it was odd that they'd adopted so soon after marriage. Barely three weeks after the wedding. But I was just a maid. I didn't ask questions. They were wholly unprepared for you, too. They had nothing. No crib, no clothes apart from what you were wearing, and that was no more than a cut-up piece of blanket. I wrapped you up warm and took you to Zhore with your mother. She bought you the best of everything that day. She might not have been prepared, but already she was in love with you."

"Why wasn't she prepared?" I asked perplexed. "Surely, if she'd adopted me, she would have gotten everything ready?"

Dahlia shrugged. "As I said, it's not really my place to say, but I got the impression that she wasn't quite expecting you."

I mulled this over. How could she not be expecting me? I didn't know much about adoption processes, but she must have known. How does anyone adopt someone without knowing? The more I thought of it, the more I realized that Dahlia was right. My mother was meticulous about everything. There was no way that she would not have had everything ready for a baby. Yet another mystery to figure out.

"What happened after that?"

"Eventually, they decided to hire a nanny, and as I'd already been looking after you, I volunteered for the job. They still wanted me as a maid, so I took on both jobs and have been doing them ever since. A few months later, your mother fell pregnant with Remy, and life went on."

She was cut off by the sound of shouting outside. Standing up, the pair of us gazed out of the window. Dahlia grabbed my shoulder and brought her free hand up to her chest. The dragons were back, and this time, they were angry.

As we watched, guards rushed at them, only for the dragons to retaliate, breathing their fire, smoking the warriors and knights.

I screamed as a group of knights got the full effect of the flames, falling to the ground, still on fire long after the dragon's fire had ended.

"Please don't let Milo be in there!" I whispered to myself, tears coursing down my cheeks.

"He set out a couple of hours ago, lovey," Dahlia assured me, gripping my shoulder tightly. I could only look on in fear as the dragons skimmed the ground, knocking over knights, burning everything in their path.

"I have to do something!" I cried, grabbing my sword from under my covers.

Dahlia's eyes widened at the sight of it.

"Now, where do you think you are going with that?"

"I'm going to fight!" I'd beaten the dragons before, and I'd do it again. Last time, I'd used magic. This time, I was going in with a sword. I'd use both if that's what it took.

"You stay right here!" Dahlia demanded. "I don't think your father would want you to..."

I didn't listen to the rest of the sentence. I was already out of the door. What I hadn't anticipated was Jack blocking my way.

"Move," I ordered sternly.

"Sorry, Your Highness, but his Majesty's orders are to keep you in here safe. Where is it you wish to go?"

"She wants to go out and fight the dragons," Dahlia told him. I could have fought him. I would have won too. He had more training than I did, but I was younger, and I was desperate. The thing was, I didn't think my father would take too kindly to his daughter killing one of his guards. Deciding against it, I ran back to my room, bolting it from the inside before Dahlia could follow. If I couldn't help on the field, maybe I could help from a distance. I'd produced a tower of fire that had made the dragons bow down before. There was nothing to say I couldn't do it again from my window. I flung the window open, just in time to see the dragons flying off into the skies. The fight was over. The pasture was littered with the bodies of men. At least twenty were burned beyond recognition. Many were injured. More still ran out to help in the fight. They would be of no use, beyond helping the injured and taking away the bodies of the dead. I scoured the men for my father. He wasn't there. Unlike Milo, who would blend in with all the others because of his uniform, my father would be easy to spot in the crowd. He wore the uniform of a king, not a guard.

A banging on my door rattled me. Pulling back the bolt, I saw Dahlia. Behind her stood Jack.

"Go and look at what has happened!" I screeched at Jack. "You are keeping me in here, but look at what is happening. Does my father even know?"

Jack strode past and glanced out of the window, his face paling from the scene below. I chose his moment of shock and ran out of the room. I wasn't going to fight anymore. There was nothing left to fight, but I would tell my father. His men needed him now more than ever.

I found him exactly where I thought he'd be, holding the hand of my mother.

"I told the guards to keep you in your room," he began when he saw me.

Out of breath, I wheezed. "The dragons have attacked. Some of your men have been killed...outside."

He stood up and strode past me out of his room. I followed along in his path, almost having to run to keep up with him. Outside in the courtyard, the non-injured men were already bringing in those that weren't so lucky. Embers floated in the air like fireflies. The injured were being brought into the castle. Those that didn't make it were being laid out next to each other. The smell of burning flesh invaded my senses, making me want to throw up, but my father stood tall. If he noticed the wretched looks on the faces of the burnt men or the stink of the charred remains, he didn't show it. He called to one of his men. When the man turned, I almost fell over in shock. It was Ash. Ash dressed in the uniform of a knight. The only distinction between his uniform and that of the others was a plume of red feathers coming out of the top of his helmet.

"Yes, Father?"

"Get someone into Zhore immediately. I want all the doctors, physicians, nurses, and healers brought up. As many as you can find. We'll also need someone to deal with the bodies. They will need identifying, and their relatives will need to know."

"Yes, sir," Ash saluted. When had all this come about? Ash was only sixteen. Why was he wearing a knight's costume, and why was he not acting like the snot-nosed kid I knew and loved?

"About the dragons?" he asked.

My father sighed. "I don't know. I had hoped that the sightings were just flukes, but now, they are killing. I always respected them and knew when to leave well enough alone, but it seems I am being forced into doing something I do not wish to do. Gather your best men, and I'll see them tomorrow about going up the mountain. You are in charge of that. I want only my best warriors up there, but they have to know what they are letting themselves in for. Get Hollis to help you. I want them all here by tomorrow. Let's sort this mess out first, though."

Ash saluted again. Hollis was here, too? He was only fifteen. Why were they knights when I was older than them? I knew they were taking the knight's training, but all this time, I thought it was just to keep them occupied.

"I'll do it, Father," I said, standing forward. "I'll go up the mountain." Fear gripped me at the thought of it, but I had a weapon no one else did. I had magic.

My father glared at me as though he'd only just realized I was still there.

"You should be in your room."

"No! If Ash and Hollis are fighting, then I want to, too. You can't lock me up because I'm a girl."

My father sighed through gritted teeth. "I'm not locking you up because you are a girl, Azia. I'm locking you up because I love you, and I don't think you are safe."

And my brothers were? Both of them had just narrowly missed being barbecued.

"But..."

"But nothing. Either go up to your room, or I will get someone to carry you up there."

I stood my ground. This wasn't the ideal time to be arguing with my father, but it was too important not to.

He nodded his head at someone behind me, and two sets of arms grabbed hold of me. I screamed and writhed against them, but these were big burly men. Even though my sword was at my side, my arms were held in such a way that I couldn't get to it.

"Make sure she gets to her room safely," My father said to them. He turned to walk away.

"Fine, I'll go to my room quietly," I screeched. "No need to have these two take me."

He turned and considered it a moment, then nodded his head.

Turning to the side, he shouted to someone who turned

out to be much worse than the two burly guards.

"Caspian, my friend. Please, will you escort Azia back to her room and make sure she doesn't get lost along the way."

Caspian looked up from one of the injured men. He was performing some kind of spell on his burned leg. As I watched, the skin on the man's leg healed. When he was done, he came towards me and took my arm.

"With pleasure."

I walked with him through the castle, my mind whirring, my nerves in tatters. It was as if my whole life was a lie. First, I was magic, and no one knew; then, I find that I'd suddenly appeared out of nowhere as a baby, and now my younger brothers were knights. Ash and Hollis, the two least knight-like people I'd ever met. Although I had to admit, I'd seen a strength in Ash's eyes I'd never seen before. Maybe he needed something like this to finally become a man. Maybe they both did. It royally sucked that I couldn't join in, though. My father had told me it was nothing to do with me being a girl, but, of course, it was. I was only a girl, fit for dresses and parties, and marrying the first guy that would have me because I was too frail to do anything alone.

Anger surged through me, and when I got to my room, I pulled my arm from Caspian's and slammed the door in his face, bolting it once again for good measure.

I could only watch on helplessly from my window as the men below did what they had to do. Far up in the skies, the dragons circled harmlessly like they had done for years.

I wondered what had changed to cause previously peaceful creatures to suddenly turn violent? It wasn't an omen, I was sure of that. It had nothing to do with superstition. Something else was at play, and I was going to find out what.

I didn't care what my father said. I would go up those mountains, and I would figure it out for myself.

*M*y stomach rumbled as I got together everything I would need for my trip. There wasn't a lot to pack, just my sword plus some warm clothes. It was cold at the bottom of the mountains. I needed to prepare myself for a lot worse at the top. If only I had burn resistant clothes, too. That would help, but in my closet of pretty dresses, I had no such thing. I could have asked Caspian to conjure me some up, but that would mean waking him at three am, and he was bound to ask questions. It was pointless, anyway. If the dragons wanted to fry me, no amount of clothes would help, fireproof or otherwise. They'd just sizzle my head instead.

With my backpack crammed with extra layers, I stole down to the kitchen. Getting past Jack had been easy. It was dark, and I'd walked quietly down the corridor in the opposite direction to where he usually sat. He'd not seen me. He was asleep. Getting out of the castle was another matter. I couldn't count on all the other guards to be asleep. As it was, the castle was almost empty. Most of the guards were out on various missions, and in a twist of irony, the worst situation the castle had been in for eighteen years meant it was at its least guarded.

I knew the kitchen staff worked early, but I hoped that three am was early enough to miss them. The kitchen was empty. I pulled some food out of the fridge and made up some sandwiches, two of which I ate. I'd barely eaten the day before, and I was starving. Food had been brought up to my room, but I was too angry and pig-headed to eat any of it. My mistake. I needed the energy to complete today's climb. I figured it would take me at least five hours to get near the top. When I got there, that's where my plan ran out. I wanted to see the dragons without them seeing me. I wanted to try and figure out what was wrong without upsetting them.

Pulling some chocolate bars and a flask of tea into my bag, I stole out of the kitchen and into the night.

I slipped out of the back gate into the woods where Milo and I had spent hours practicing sword fighting. I only hoped that all that practice would come in handy. Fingering my sword to make sure it was still there, I felt a moment of reassurance. I strode through the woods purposefully, not daring to stop or even to consider how dangerous my plan was. I should have left it up to my father's men, but I knew that it was something more than an omen or the dragons coming down the mountain for no reason. In my heart, I knew something much deeper was in play, and the only way to figure it out was to head up the mountain. My father's men would go in there, all noise and bluster, and get themselves killed without being any closer to finding out what was going on. I might not have a set plan, but I knew I would play this a lot more carefully than any man in a suit of armor could do. I was not only going to come out of this alive, I was going to come out of it a hero, and if I had to kill a dragon or two...well, so be it.

At least, that's what I told myself as I crept up to the wall, blocking me from the mountain. I could have tried to come up with a way to climb over it, but I could see in the distance that it had not yet been completed. Of course, it hadn't. It would take months to surround the mountain, and many of those tasked to the job had been sent out to look for a spindle instead.

Finding a way up the first part of the mountain was easy. Paths worn away by generations of hikers drifted up the first part of the way. They didn't go very far. Even before the dragons decided to come down to the moors, hikers were not stupid enough to venture very far. Pretty soon, I was higher than the castle, and I could see for miles. Snow-covered most of Draconis, so I couldn't get a good view of the normally red and purple landscape, but I could see Zhore in the distance with a number of other small villages dotted around. Seeing the kingdom before me made me think of Milo. He was out there somewhere. I'd been so worried about him leaving, but the truth was, he was much safer than me. While he was asking old ladies about spindles, I was out conquering dragons. As long as he didn't run into Derillen, which I doubted he would, he would be fine. Caspian was adamant that the woman in the wool shop couldn't possibly be Derillen, but I knew in my heart it was.

The gradient steepened as the terrain of the mountain changed. Snow-covered heather gave way to grey, craggy rocks, which I would have to climb. I pulled myself from rock to rock, finding paths when and where I could. Mostly, it was just scrambling rather than full-on rock climbing, but I had the snow and ice to deal with, too, which made every foothold treacherous. After three hours of climbing, I took a break and pulled out one of the chocolate bars I'd pilfered from the kitchen. I was still a couple of hours from the top of the mountain, but I wasn't taking any risks after what I'd seen the day before, so I sat under a rocky outcrop and tore open the chocolate. A blanket of snow covered Draconis, but the sky was clear, and the sunrise gave the blanket of snow a pinkish glow. Taking in my surroundings, I noticed a small door, incongruous to the landscape around it. I was curious until I realized what it was. I'd never seen one before, but I'd heard of them. It was a dwarf door, one of many hidden on the mountainside. The main entrance to the dwarf mines lay about five miles east of the castle, but the mines themselves stretched out throughout the Fire Mountains. These doors allowed access to and from the mines, whether for emergencies or just for the dwarves to admire the view, I did not know, but I knew to leave well enough alone. I was already on my way to fight one creature; I didn't want to start a fight with other creatures too.

For a start, they had more weapons than I did. Putting the chocolate wrapper back in my bag, I set off again. The incline was getting steeper, and my going was slower. With each step, my lungs strained, and my muscles burned like dragon breath. The air was thinner up here, something that I'd not thought about when I planned this little quest. Breathing became something I had to think about something I had to consciously put effort into rather than something I just did. At the rate I was going, I would end up killing myself, long before the dragons got to me. If I didn't expire from lack of oxygen, I was likely to slip on an icy rock and fall to my death.

I was just beginning to think this whole thing was a bad idea when a brilliant blue dragon flew right over my head. It circled around before coming in again, and this time, it dove right towards me.

I grunted at the force of the dragon's talons as it gripped me, pinning my arms to the side. The little air I'd managed to breathe left me as it squeezed tighter. We flew upwards, going at a much quicker pace than I had managed alone.

I struggled in its grip, straining to get air into my lungs as the smell of burning and sulfur filled my nose.

When it had reached its destination, it dropped me. I fell only two or three feet, but the shock of it had me tumbling over and over. Something blocked my path, causing me to come to a standstill. For a second, I felt relief until I saw what I'd come up against. It was the leg of another dragon. A dragon that was craning its head around to see me.

My heart beat so quickly, I could feel the rush of blood through my eardrums, and a shiver went down my spine. Looking around, I realized I was in some kind of hollow. A thrill of fear passed through me as I saw bones littering it. Big bones. Scrambling to my feet, I ran, trying to get away from the beast. In a riot of storm and smoke, other dragons, ten or more of them, circled around what I could only describe as a giant nest, all of them fixated on me. None of them moved in to attack. They just watched intently as I pulled myself up the curved edge of the nest to the rim. When I looked over, it became apparent why none of them had gone for me. I was hundreds of feet up with a steep drop below me. A fall would kill me instantly. I was in a dragon's nest, and not only was I their dinner, it seemed they were going to play with me first.

Turning, I saw the dragon I'd originally backed into. A huge red beast with long eyelashes and big teeth, although its mouth was closed. With my back to the rim of the nest, there was nowhere for me to go. My options were to jump over the edge to my death or to stay and have it eat me alive, burned to death, or pulled apart by sharp talons. None of those options appealed, but as fear was gripping me to the floor of the nest, it seemed my nervous system would decide for me.

"Dragon balls," I hissed, pulling myself right to the edge. Below me, another couple of dragons flew. They were so low down that they looked tiny, and yet from the castle, they looked so high up. My hand gripped the edge, and something cold touched against it. My sword! I had my sword. I also had magic. Magic had saved me from the dragons before, it could do it again, but while I dialed back my nerves, the sword would have to do. Pulling it out, I leveled it at the red dragon. Immediately, the surrounding dragons flew closer, but the red dragon shot warning looks at them, and they flew back again. Was it warning them off so it could eat me itself?

Remembering my stance, I moved cautiously towards the dragon. It watched me closely but made no move. It could have roasted me at any point, but it chose not to, and when I was within hitting distance of it, and it still hadn't moved, I was left immobile with indecision. My nerves had dropped a little. If I'd wanted to, I could have reached forward and pet its snout. I was here to kill it, or at least I thought I was, but no. I'd come up here to understand the dragons. I couldn't understand anything if I killed them. It blinked as I stood right in front of it, probably wondering what my next move would be.

You and me both, buddy, I thought.

I didn't know what to do, but killing it was no longer an option. I could kill in self-defense, but I could never attack something that was not attacking me. Instead, I did the unthinkable. I put my sword away and bridged the distance between us. Taking a last step, I held out my hand and touched the tip of its nose. It closed its eyes and then opened them again. This creature was no threat to me.

"We wondered when you would come to see us."

My heart pelted around my chest at the voice behind me. There had been no one in this nest a minute ago, I was sure of it. I turned to find a man, or at least, he was almost a man. The top half of his body was human if you could call a man with long blue hair human. Brilliant blue scales that shimmered in the sun covered his bottom half. His legs were the legs of a dragon, and I knew this was the dragon that had brought me up here.

"You are a...What are you?" I'd asked the fae the same question only a week ago. He didn't take too kindly to it. Hopefully, this man would understand my confusion. Unlike Caspian, who had growled at the question, this man smiled widely in response. He came forward and held his hand out for me to shake.

"I am Vasuki, the king of the dragons, and you are my new queen."

I must have stood there, my mouth hanging open, because he carried on talking.

"Things in your world are changing, and in turn, they affecting ours."

"I can't be your queen," I bleated. "I'm already in a fake relationship with someone I've inadvertently developed a crush on, and I'm almost, not quite, but probably engaged to someone else. My love life is tangled enough without turning my weird love triangle into a love square."

Vasuki laughed, though there was no joy in it. "I apologize for laughing, but you misunderstand me. I am already with a partner. Although we do not follow the human constructs of marriage, I am very much partnered with her for life, and she is the love of my life. I do not wish for your body, nor your soul. I only wish your council and your magic."

"I'm not too sure I can give you those either," I said, confusion in every word. "Can you tell me what is going on?"

He moved forward and took my hand. He was so unthreatening that I let him. On my other side, my other hand was taken by someone else. It was the red dragon with the huge eyelashes, but now she was a beautiful woman, or at least, half-woman for she was scaled from the waist down like Vasuki. Her hair was a magnificent crop of ombre, ranging from orange at the root to flaming red at the ends.

The pair of them were so beautiful, they took my breath away, and the sooty smell followed them, even after their change.

"This is Emba," He said, introducing the red-headed woman to me. She smiled a dazzling smile and nodded her head slightly.

"Things are changing in your world," Vasuki repeated. "Normally, we do not care about the goings-on of humans, but unfortunately, it has invaded our world. Not once have we allowed a human up here, but you are different. We are hoping...I am hoping that you will do us a service."

I pulled back from the two of them, remembering the charred remains of the guards being lined up in the castle grounds.

"You killed people," I choked. "You killed the castle guards. My father is gearing his men up to come and attack you."

Vasuki threw a knowing look at Emba before turning back to me. "That was not us...at least, it was none of my doing. Please hear me out. I am no threat to you, nor is my dragon clan. I will promise you safety and safe passage back down the mountain if you listen to what I have to say. It is as important for you as it is for us."

I nodded my head slowly. It was hardly as if I had any choice in the matter, but I let that slide. I was intrigued by what he had to say.

"A couple of weeks ago, a massive shift in magical energy occurred. I doubt if humans felt it, but magical beings are sensitive to such things and dragons probably more so than most. I feared that things would go back to how they were many years ago. I felt a darkness that was all too familiar to me. I hoped that it was nothing, that the change was just some natural shift in energy, but then the humans started coming. Many years ago, we were hunted almost into extinction. Humans were afraid, angry. People were hurting other people, all because of the darkness, and they didn't stop there. Greed was prevalent. Humans came up the mountain. They stole from the mines, and they stole eggs from us and hunted us as trophies. The darkness affected us too, and we began to fight back. It was only when the princess of the people woke up from a slumber that things got better for us. Her father, the king, made the journey up the mountain himself and made it clear that he was outlawing dragon hunting. He told us we would be free, and as long as we stayed on the mountaintops, no one would bother us again. He was true to his word until the darkness came back a couple of weeks ago. The humans blamed us, although we know no more about it than they do."

"The king was my grandfather," I told him. "The princess who slept is my mother. She is cursed once again and now lies in slumber at the castle."

A curious look passed between Vasuki and the red dragon.

"That cannot be," he said, confusion in his voice. "You are not the same as him."

"I'm adopted," I explained. "My parents adopted me eighteen years ago."

Comprehension dawned. "Ah, I see. That makes sense. You are a lucky woman. Your grandfather is a good man."

"My grandfather died many years ago."

Vasuki bowed his head. "I'm sorry to hear that. My condolences. We do not keep up with what happens down there unless it affects us directly. As I said, it became illegal to hunt dragons, and until now, we have not been harmed. Unfortunately, in the past two weeks we have had many instances of humans coming up the mountain. Our eggs are being stolen again. Lives are being lost. I wanted to come down and speak to your grandfather, but my kind is not welcome down there, as you can imagine. I had planned to wait a week or so more, keeping extra guard over our eggs, but some of the dragons disobeyed my orders and took it upon themselves to give the humans a warning. I did not ask them to do it, and they will be punished for their actions. I do not believe in an eye for an eye. That way, everyone ends up blind. We are a peaceful people and do not wish to harm humans."

"My father has been erecting a wall to keep people off the mountain, but it will take months to build, even with all the men he has available."

Vasuki smiled curtly. "It seems your father is a good man as well. Please tell him we mean no harm, but we cannot have more humans on the mountain. I will talk to the dragons responsible for killing your guards, and I will make it clear that I don't want it to happen again, but I cannot chain them down. They are angry and mistrustful of humans. The dark energy is making everyone edgy."

"I can understand why," I said. "I'm sorry that we humans are doing this to you. I can ask the media to tell the people you are shifters. I doubt anyone would want to steal your eggs if they knew that."

Vasuki shook his head roughly. "That is where you are wrong. Dragon eggs are valuable, but Dragon shifter eggs are the most valuable of all. We are a rare species, and our eggs are priceless in certain markets. Only your grandfather knew the truth about us. I have to trust that you will keep our secret and only tell your father and no one else."

I nodded. "If you are sure."

"I am sure." He paused before speaking again. "May I ask you why you came up to see us? I see that you are carrying a sword that bears our image. A high honor, indeed, although I would expect nothing less from our queen."

There he went again calling me his queen. He had yet to explain why. "I came up for information. I had a feeling that you had something to do with the shift in magical energy, but now I know you do not. Why do you keep referring to me as your queen?"

Milo had called me the queen of dragons a few times, and now it seemed he wasn't wrong. The irony of it didn't escape me.

"Do you not feel it?" he asked, gazing at the air around him.

I felt a lot of things at the moment, but whatever it was he was referring to, no, I didn't.

I shrugged, not knowing how to answer.

"You have a very deep connection to us," he said. "The magical ability you showed the other day drew our kind down from the mountain. You called to us. There is something I must tell you that you may not already understand. You said earlier that you were sorry that we humans did this to you. That's how you phrased it. We humans. You are not human. You are something much greater."

I blinked, unnerved by his words. "What do you mean I'm not human?"

I mean, what else could I be? I looked human, I talked like a human, I walked like a human. I'd already established that I wasn't fae and there was no way I was a witch or a vampire. He was wrong. he had to be wrong...but...

Caspian had said something similar. I was magic, a skill that humans didn't possess except the mages of Enchantia. Was it possible I was from there originally? Why would my parents adopt me from a place so far away when there were plenty of orphans here in Draconis? But then, I couldn't be a mage either if Vasuki was right. Mages were human. He was saying I wasn't.

"My eyes!" The gold ring around my irises had always marked me apart from others.

"Yes, your eyes are unusual." It was Emba who spoke. I'd

not heard her speak before. Her voice was rich like honey, and she had the same accent as Vasuki." I have never seen anything like them. We do not know what you are, but we know you are special. It is foreseen that you will bring prosperity to our kind."

"Foreseen?"

She nodded. "We have a limited sense of the future. We do not see things as such, but we feel the vibrations rippling back. We are in for dark times, but there is a hint of the light in the distance. We believe that you are part of that. We feel a great affinity to you, one that has nothing to do with the fact that you are royalty."

"Indeed," Vasuki agreed. "We would not have known your royal status unless you told us. You are a queen of the people, as well as a queen of dragons. We bow down to you."

"I don't understand," I said.

"Neither do I," Vasuki admitted. "I cannot answer your questions, and I am sorry. All I can tell you is that your magic draws us to you. You are very special to us though I don't even understand it fully myself. We rarely bow down to others, but our bond with you is strong."

As he spoke, the other dragons that had been circling flew in and dropped their bellies to the ground as they did before. Looking around, the sight baffled me, but I now felt a kinship with them I'd never thought possible. Not that I'd thought dragon shifters were possible either. Just then, a smaller dragon nudged me harmlessly in the back of my leg with its snout. It was the most beautiful dragon I'd ever seen with brilliant iridescent purple scales that changed color in the sunlight. It looked up at me with mischievous eyes and made a cute little barking growl sound.

"Yes, Nyre," said Vasuki to the little dragon. He pronounced the name Ny-ree. "You may take her back, but fly straight back, you hear? Don't go too close to the castle.

You won't be safe, but your small size will make it harder for the castle guards to see you."

The small dragon half-hopped, half-flew up and rested on my shoulder. It was barely bigger than a puppy. How was it supposed to fly me down the mountain?

The red dragon stood back up from her kneeling position and kissed my hand. "My daughter has always had a fascination with the human world, and even though you are not human, you are still part of it. I think she likes you. It would be a great honor to us if you let her take you down the mountain."

"You mean, fly on her back?" I asked, looking at the small purple dragon on my shoulder nervously. I doubted I'd fit on its back.

"No. Nyre will know what to do. She is a proficient flyer and stronger than she looks." Vasuki said. "I trust that you will pass on my sincere condolences at what my brethren did to your people. I will do my utmost to stop it from happening again. If your father is building a wall, I will pass the message on to the perpetrators. If he and his men come up the mountain, I will set defenses, but will not attack first. I will, however, fight back if need be."

I nodded as Nyre nudged me again. She hopped up and down on my shoulder impatiently. "I will keep your secret too."

"Thank you. You are welcome here whenever you want, but the rest of your people are not. Be safe, young princess."

Before I had time to answer him, Nyre's talons bit into my backpack, pulling me into the sky. All I could do was grip onto the straps of the backpack and hope neither of them broke.

I'd expected a calm flight down the base of the mountains, but Nyre had other ideas. She flew with me in the opposite direction, over the peaks of the mountains. I should have felt scared, but like Vasuki had said, I shared an affinity with her as if I could almost read her thoughts. She didn't want to hurt me; she wanted to show me things. She wanted to have fun. I whooped as she spun into a dive before leveling out. My heart raced almost as much as Nyre did, but I was having the time of my life. The view was like nothing I'd ever seen before, and I saw parts of Draconis that I'd never been to. Red mountains emerged out of the snow, giving me the most impressive scenery. We flew for hours, over secluded villages and hidden valleys, and before I knew it, the sun was beginning to lower in the sky.

"I have to get home," I said to her, and she nodded, before turning in mid air. My stomach rumbled. I had food in my back pack, but as she was holding on to it, I couldn't get to it to eat and so by the time I could see the castle, I was starving. She came into land at the other side of the woods where no one would see her. No doubt there would be men on patrol looking out for dragons and the woods was the safest place I could think for her to land.

I'd only just touched down when an arrow flew past me, almost grazing my ear. Nyre launched herself from my back, taking off into the sky, flying quickly away as more arrows followed her.

"Stop it," I shouted at the shadow in the woods. I couldn't see who it was, but I could clearly see the bow in his hands.

The man stepped forward out of the woods. "Azia?"

My heart skipped a beat when I realised who it was. "Father?"

"Get back to the castle at once!" He demanded, pointing sharply at the path through the woods that would lead me back home.

"But I have something to tell you," I began, but he cut me off.

"At once!" he barked. "Don't make me repeat myself again."

He marched behind me as I walked, not letting me speak at all. When we got to my room he opened the door for me.

"I've been out looking for you all day," He hissed as I walked past him. "Don't you think I have better things to do than go looking for you? Your mother is sick, the people are frightened, my guards don't know what to do next and that's only the ones that survived the dragon attack."

His voice got louder and louder with each syllable.

"I couldn't deal with any of it. I couldn't be there to comfort the bereaved families and I had no time to organise a killing trip up the mountains, and why? Because of you!"

He shouted the last word.

"Jack," he barked. "Come here. I want you standing outside this door all night. she is not to come out at all, do you understand?"

He slammed the door shut behind me, leaving me trapped in my very own prison, with no hope of escape.

I'd not even had the chance to beg him not to go up the mountains and kill the dragons.

I found out very quickly that not even Dahlia was allowed to come to my room to visit. My father himself brought me my food, but he wouldn't stay long enough to let me talk. The strain in his face was evident as he dropped the tray of food on my side table before slamming the door shut behind him. I could do nothing but stare out of the window and wait for the men to return, men which included both my brothers. My brothers aged fifteen and sixteen. It boiled my blood that Ash and Hollis were out there, doing something important for our kingdom and they weren't even of age yet and here I was, the heir to the throne, locked in my room and engaged to someone I didn't even like.

As if he could sense my grumbling (and yes, he probably could) Caspian knocked on my door in the early afternoon. I opened it quickly.

"What do you want?" I asked, not even bothering to put on any airs and graces. He was about as welcome as dragon rot.

"I came to see how you were and bring you chocolate."

"Great," I said, snatching the chocolate bar from his hand. At that point I would have liked to slam the door in his face, but he'd managed to sidle past it and was already in my room.

I didn't say anything. I guess I was too annoyed with everything else going on to care about my feelings towards him. Sitting down on the bed, I tore off the chocolate wrapper and tore a chunk of chocolate with my teeth.

"I came to tell you that I've started arrangements for our wedding. It will be a glorious affair."

My heart dropped further at his words. I'd been so caught up in everything else, I'd not even thought about the wedding. Who even cared about a wedding when my father was starting a war with the dragons and my mother was cursed and Milo was out there looking for a witch. It kinda made the thought of wedding favours and bridesmaid dresses seem ridiculous.

"I'm not doing it." I replied plainly, laying back on the bed. "It's a ridiculous notion."

"Your father doesn't think so," Caspian argued, sitting on the end of my bed.

I grimaced at him. "My father is not himself. He doesn't know what he's doing. He doesn't really care if I marry you or not, he's only making me do it because my mother is cursed and he thinks that's what she wants."

"But he is making you do it," Caspian countered.

I sat up to face him, bringing my feet up away from him. "My mother and father barely know you. You helped my father all those years ago, but you said yourself that the curse was already beginning to wane so in reality you did nothing. You did nothing then and you are doing nothing now."

"On the contrary," he replied, inching slightly closer. Any closer and I was going to kick him off the bed. "I've been to see your mother. I saw her when she first fell into the curse, but last night your father asked me to perform some spells to see what was wrong. I wanted to see if there was anything I could do to help her."

The tightness I'd been carrying around in my chest lightened considerably at his words. "And could you?" I held my breath. If anyone could help her it was him.

He licked his lips as he thought how to word what he was about to say. "It is indeed a curse that is binding her to sleep, but I don't think it's as simple as that. She is not just sleeping. I believe she is bound to the Dream Realm."

I raised a brow. "Dream Realm?"

"We all dream," he said. "Most of us about banal things. Occasionally we have strange dreams. I myself once dreamed I turned into a toad.

"If only," I retorted through gritted teeth. "Get to the point."

"It's these strange dreams we have that take us into the Dream Realm. Unlike the normal dreams of family or whatever, the strange dreams are like postcards of our visit to another world. It is a place that many visit without realising it's real. Very few stay more than a few minutes. We wake and the Dream Realm falls away. Whoever cursed your mother put up a block when she was in the Dream Realm. Stopped her from exiting. That, I believe is how this particular curse works."

I tried to get my head around what he was telling me.

"So she is in another world, lost?"

He shook his head "I doubt she is lost. This is a world she knows well. She spent a hundred years there already. She just can't find the exit."

I heaved a deep sigh. I had a choice, either believe the lying toe-rag or throw him out of my room. As I had very little else to do with my time beyond lay on my bed and grumble about my situation, I decided to hear him out.

"She's never mentioned another world before," I said, pulling my feet even closer to me.

This time he didn't follow. "I bet she hasn't. The Dream Realm is not a nice place. There are no rules there and the landscape is made up of other people's imaginations."

"So it isn't real then?"

"Oh, it's very real," he insisted. "It will feel as real to your mother than the real world does to you. She will be able to see, hear, smell, touch. Much of it will be familiar to her as she will have formed a lot of it with her own mind. Just because it's constantly evolving, doesn't mean it's not real. I'm not a master of the art of sleep, but I know someone who is. She studied Morpheus at the university in Urbis."

"Who's Morpheus?"

"Morpheus," Caspian said, "Is the god of sleep and dreams. The Dream Realm is his domain. He likes his fun...his dark fun."

Our kingdom had many gods that people worshipped, and I didn't believe in a single one of them. I'd never heard of Morpheus. Maybe Caspian was making this all up so I'd marry him. I wouldn't put it past him. The whole thing sounded like total boohickey.

"If the Dream Realm exists," I asked, uncertainty in my voice. "What's to stop me, or anyone else from going in there in our sleep and pulling my mother back?"

"It doesn't work like that."

No, of course it didn't. Why would anything be so simple?

"Morpheus is a trickster," he stated, staring right into my eyes, giving me an involuntary shiver. "The person you see in there might be your mother, but it also might be a trick by Morpheus. He's not a nice guy and yet he's a God so there's nothing anyone can do. If your mother is trapped in his world, whoever did it must know him. He wouldn't trap anyone without someone very close to him asking him to, but once he has them, he'll play with them."

Bile burned at the back of my throat. If he wasn't telling me this as some weird joke, the thought of it was horrific. It was hard enough knowing my mother was a sleep, but knowing she was also trapped in some kind of Dream Realm with a crazy god made everything a lot worse.

"Derillen?"

Caspian shook his head. "I know you've said it before, but I don't think Derillen is the person behind your mother's sleep this time. I think it's a copy cat. The person you think you saw was copying her. Anyone could get a horned head-dress made up."

"Think I saw? I did see her and I don't understand how this is so hard for you to believe."

Caspian sighed. "I really didn't want to get into this with you. Derillen went a long time ago. She was extremely powerful. Probably the most powerful witch that ever lived. No one could defeat her, not even me."

"Which makes it more likely that the witch I saw is her."

"Actually, I think it means the opposite. Something defeated her back then. She was relentless. She wouldn't just disappear without someone making her. I just don't know who. I can't think of anyone with that much power. She took it from the gods themselves. I think Morpheus knew her and told someone else how to block the exits to the Dream Realm."

"I need to get my mother out, Caspian," I whispered, swallowing back the lump in my throat.

He brought his hand to his chin thoughtfully. "There is a way to get into the Dream Realm from ours but I do not know it. My friend studied dream lore for a long time. I could ask her to come here."

Hope rose in my chest. "Could you?"

He nodded "I will send word to her, but she will not be able to get here soon. She lives in Urbis. It's quite a journey, even on the Urbis Express."

I thought of the huge sky ships that occasionally passed by in the distant sky. I'd never travelled on one, but I'd often wondered how nice it would be to travel so high up, to see the kingdom from above. I'd had a taste of it by flying on Nyre yesterday and I wanted more.

"I appreciate it, thank you."

Caspian took my hand and for the first time, I didn't pull away.

"I owe you for everything I've done to you," he said. "What I did was wrong. I wanted your mother to like me and I wanted to marry you. I shouldn't have betrayed your trust, just to get what I wanted, but I didn't know what else to do. I hoped that if I could only get you to marry me, then maybe love would come after."

"Tell me honestly," I started, looking right into his eyes. "You talk of love and specifically of my love, but you never talk of your own. Do you love me?"

He looked at me intently, those amethyst eyes boring into me. "I cannot say I feel love. I barely know you, but I feel a connection and I feel a strong attraction to you that I wasn't prepared for. I came here to help your father out. I wasn't expecting to even like you, let alone love you, but I've seen things in you that I've never seen in anyone else. You have a bravery like no one I've ever known. Your father told me that he caught you flying in the talons of a dragon yesterday. I cannot even begin to understand how you managed something so dangerous without getting hurt or killed. I also cannot comprehend why you would want to do something so reckless, especially after what the dragons did to your father's men."

I sighed. "Is my father still mad at me?"

"Of course he is. Would you expect anything different?" he arched a brow waiting for my answer.

"The dragons aren't as bad as everyone thinks," I said, remembering my talk with Vasuki the day before.

"All evidence to the contrary."

"Just because some dragons hurt my father's men, doesn't mean that they all did." I wanted to tell him about Vasuki and the others but I'd been asked not to and Caspian had betrayed me once too often for me to trust him completely.

"No, maybe not, but they've done enough damage. I know they are fascinating creatures. I, myself would like to know more about them, but that doesn't mean you should put your life at risk to study them. Maybe their behaviour is directly related to your mother's curse, maybe not, but killing yourself to find out won't help the kingdom and it won't help your mother. You are best staying in here where your father knows you are safe until this all passes."

I sighed. "I don't want to stay in here. I'm being punished. I don't want to be a princess locked in a tower, waiting for a knight to save me. I want to be the knight and I want to save everyone else."

"And that..." Caspian said, standing up, "is half the problem. That's the reason your father won't let you out. He can't trust that you won't go and do something crazy like you did yesterday. I have something for you. I didn't want to give it to you like this, but I don't see there being a better time in the next three weeks."

He bent down to his knee and produced a box. When he opened it, I saw the most gorgeous ring in white gold with a huge amethyst set in the middle of it. It was the amethyst from his sword. The one I'd thrown from my bedroom window in the previous week.

"I don't want to ask you to marry me, I already know your

answer, but I hope you'll wear it anyway. It belonged to my mother."

When I didn't move or speak, he left the box on my bed and walked to the door.

"I'll speak to my friend about Morpheus," he promised and then left, shutting the door quietly behind him.

Picking up the box, I laid back on the bed. It really was a beautiful ring. My mother would love it. I thought back to what Caspian had said about Morpheus. I'd never heard the name before, just as I'd not heard of Derillen before last week. There was so much happening, so many new names, so many people involved and yet none of it really was new. This had all been in play before I was born and instead of coming to an end, had merely been paused, ready to start again, bringing the horrors back.

Derillen was where this had all started. I'd learned her name. I'd even seen her and yet I knew nothing about her. My mother had never really talked about her life before her big sleep. The story of my father meeting her and saving her eclipsed everything that came before and whenever I'd asked her about it, she'd brushed it off saying it didn't matter anymore. But it did matter. If only I'd pushed her on the subject, maybe I'd have an idea how to solve all these problems now. If I could get to Derillen and stop the darkness she was spreading, everything else would fall into place.

I slipped the ring on my finger. It fitted perfectly. Of course it did, I expected no less from Caspian

Sighing, I pulled it off and placed it back in the box that I put on my nightstand. I couldn't think about weddings and rings. My mother was still cursed and the kingdom was falling apart. I didn't even know if my father's men had attacked the dragons. I'd been watching from my bedroom window, and I'd not seen anyone venturing up the Fire

Mountains, but that didn't mean they hadn't. It only meant that I'd not seen them.

I closed my eyes and wished for sleep even though I wasn't tired. I needed to know if Caspian's story about the Dream Realm was true. It took over an hour of tossing and turning, but eventually the darkness eclipsed the light and I found myself dreaming. I was flying with Nyre again but below me the kingdom was strange and distorted.

"Go down there," I whispered and Nyre fell into a dive so steep I had to hold on for dear life. We hurtled towards the ground at an astonishing speed. It was too quick. We were going to crash. I fell out of my bed with a scream.

My door opened.

"Azia, what happened?"

I stood, blinking the sleep from my eyes. Milo stood before me. After a moment of confusion, I saw that he was real and the Dream Realm had escaped me. I fell into his arms, exhaustion passing through me. Tears prickled my eyes.

He brought his thumb up and wiped them away.

"What's going on?"

Looking over Milo's shoulder I saw Jack watching us.

"It's okay Jack. I've got this," Milo said, following my line of sight to the old guard.

"His majesty won't approve," Jack huffed.

"It's okay Jack," I said, pulling Milo into my room. "Milo's job is to protect me. I won't be able to run away while he's here."

"That's not what I was worried ab..."

"Bye Jack." I closed the door and pulled the bolt across for good measure.

"You shouldn't have done that," Milo said, keeping his voice low. I smiled for the first time all day.

"I know, and I know I don't care. I'm just glad to have you

back." I pulled him into a hug and immediately my fears fell away. Everything felt better when Milo was around, even if nothing really had changed.

He held me tightly, running his hand up and down my back, comforting me. I never wanted to let go, but if Jack was to tell my father that Milo was here, he'd be right up here demanding Milo leave.

I pulled apart from him and sat down on the bed. "Did you find any spindles?"

Milo shook his head in frustration. "No. Not one. The whole thing was a waste of time. I've spent the last two days terrifying elderly ladies while I searched through their houses on order of your father. No one has any spindles anymore. If the witch has one, she is long gone and has taken it with her. It was more than likely made out of magic anyway and if it was, we will never find it. I spent the whole time thinking about you."

"You did?"

He nodded and took my hand in his. His face was pale, lined with worry. "There's something I have to tell you and I don't know how."

His shoulder slumped as if the weight of the world was upon him. A thrill of fear ran through me.

"What is it?"

"I was in the teams scouting around Zhore and the other nearby towns. That's why I'm back so soon. I didn't have too far to go. Here..." He pulled out a copy of a newspaper and handed it over.

It was the Draconian Sentinel, the Draconis national paper. I'd not read the paper in days and now that I could see the headline, I realised why. It had been hidden from me. It was an announcement of Caspian and my wedding on the date my father had said. My hand went to my throat as I read the announcement. The whole kingdom was invited to a party I knew nothing about, to which I was the main guest. I threw the paper down in frustration.

"He gave me a ring today," I said pointing to the box that still sat on the nightstand. He must have known about this announcement and didn't say anything. "

I stood up and paced the room. "Why are they reporting this when the whole kingdom is falling to pieces?"

"I don't understand it either," Milo said. He sounded so defeated. "I thought that the dragons would take up more column space but I suspect that your father has something to do with this. Maybe he thinks that the kingdom needs something to look forward to. Zhore is already preparing for the party. The town square was being decorated when I left."

"I don't want to marry him."

"I know," Milo replied softly. He stood up to face me and pulled me to him. "And I'm not going to let you. I told you I'd fight for you before and I meant it. If the law states that a suitor can win your hand in competition, then I'll fight for you. I know what I said when I left, but I was wrong. I missed you so much and realised what an ass I'd been. I'll always fight for you."

I'd completely forgotten about the book that Remy had shown me. So much had happened since then. I guess I thought that my father wouldn't push a wedding on me with so much already going on. How wrong I was.

"Azia." Milo looked right at me. "I don't want to lose you. I know we barely know each other and I know that I don't have a ring or the blessing of the king, but if I win this competition, will you marry me?"

It was my second proposal in just over two hours. It was probably a kingdom-wide record. I'd gone over eighteen years without anyone being interested in me and now I had two men, both of which I'd only just met, willing to fight for my hand in marriage. Well Milo was, but I guessed that

Caspian wouldn't want to lose face. He was a warrior. He would fight too.

"Wait here," I said, unbolting the door.

I strode right past Jack who tried stopping me.

"You are not to leave the room," he said, holding his sword up.

"Don't you think that's overkill, Jack?" Milo said behind me.

"No, not really," Jack replied. "She sneaked past me once already. I can't let it happen again. The king will have my job."

I pushed the sword away from my chest with my finger. He was all bluster. My father would be much more upset if one of his guards turned me into Swiss cheese than if I got out of my room again. "It's my father I'm going to see," I said to him. Please come with me if you don't believe me."

Poor Jack looked nervous as I strode purposefully past him. I didn't turn around, but I could hear two sets of footsteps following me. One from Jack who didn't trust me and one from Milo who had ignored my order to stay where he was. I'd not wanted him with me when I confronted my father and demanded a competition, but as I walked I realised it made sense for Milo to be there. Technically anyone could enter, but only Milo and Caspian would.

I didn't want to have a competition. I was too busy. I had the dragons to worry about, not to mention this Morpheus character that Caspian mentioned, that I still wasn't sure was real or not. But if I didn't at least propose a competition, my father would have me married off before I had chance to do anything about either of those problems, and despite everything that Caspian said, He'd probably keep me at home like a good little wife.

My first stop was my father's bedroom, but it was empty save for my sleeping mother and her own maid.

"I'm looking for my father," I said to the maid. "Do you know where he is?"

She shuffled her feet nervously. "I believe he is in the main hall talking to his men. A lot of them are back today."

I nodded my thanks and once again brushed past Jack.

He looked no happier to be following me than I was of having him follow me.

I found my father exactly where the maid said he was.

The great hall was filled with men but the overall atmosphere was one of defeat. None of these men had found a spindle and they never would.

I saw Caspian in the corner talking to one of the men. When he looked up, I beckoned him over.

"Did you send word to your friend yet?" I asked.

"Of course. As soon as I left your room.." His eyes flickered down to my hand.

"I see you are not wearing my ring yet."

"Actually, that's why I'm here," I said. "Please come with me."

My father seemed surprised to find his daughter with three men in tow. "What's this?"

"I tried to stop her sire, but she's a wilful one," Jack pointed out.

My father sighed. "And that's exactly why I asked you to guard her." To my side, Jack sunk back. I would have felt sorry for him if he wasn't so intent about keeping me locked in my room.

"I do not want to marry Caspian," I said. I turned to Caspian. "I'm sorry. The ring you gave me is truly spectacular, but I cannot marry you because you gave me nice jewellery."

"Not this again," My father huffed. "I'm well aware of your thoughts on the matter. Indeed, you've not stopped telling me them , but as I've already told you, you have no choice and I do not wish to discuss this matter with you again. As you can see I'm extremely busy with my men. As soon as they all get back from looking for spindles I'm sending them up the mountains."

"I do have a choice and it's the law," I said, standing my ground. I brought my hands up to my hips. "Remy found it in a book."

My father raised an eyebrow? "What has Remy got to do with this?"

"Everything! He found a book of old Draconis laws. One of them states that if there is more than one suitor for the heir to the throne, a competition should be held to decide between them.

"More than one suitor?" My father blustered. It was clear that he didn't want to be having this conversation, but tough luck, because I was going to have my say. "That's preposterous," he added.

"I agree," Interjected Caspian, pushing forward. "I'm the only person that has asked you to marry me!"

"Actually, that's not quite true," Milo said, standing forward. "I just asked her."

Caspian's face dropped. "You can't."

"He can," I said. "I never accepted your proposal. You gave me a ring, but you can see for yourself that I'm not wearing it. I've not accepted any proposal and seeing as my father would not let me accept one from Milo, it will have to go to competition."

My father brought his hand up to the back of his neck and closed his eyes. "I don't know of this law. I've never heard of it." He spoke through gritted teeth.

Just then, Remy's voice echoed through the hall.

"Aza!" He ran towards us, the book of laws in his hand. He passed it to my father.

"Page thirty two," I said, a self satisfied smile on my face. I gave Remy a wink who beamed at me.

My father turned the pages.

Casplan bridged the gap between him and my father. "You can't listen to this Alec? Just because something is written in an old book doesn't mean it's true. Besides you are the king. You make the laws."

My father found the right page and read it quickly.

"It's true, I do make the laws..." he said, slowly.

"But it's Urbis that passes them," I added, raising my eyebrows in triumph. "And changes in law can take months...years even." I folded my arms and gave Caspian a smirk.

Beside me, my father sighed. "Fine. If this is the law, then so be it. We will have a competition but let it be known that I'm not happy about this. I have way too much to deal with, without this nonsense too."

"You could just let me wait until I'm ready to be married then pick who I want," I said.

He shook his head. "No. The wedding will go ahead. It's already booked." He looked to Caspian. "I trust you can win this."

He then snapped at one of the guards who ran right over.

"Go to the editor of the Draconian Sentinel and let him know that the wedding is still on, but we don't know the groom yet. Tell him that the last post was a mistake. You'd better tell him that we are abiding by law and holding a competition for the princess's hand in marriage."

He threw me a look of agitation and threw the book back to Remy before storming out of the room. Caspian followed, trying to get him to change his mind.

"Good job Remy," I said, pulling my brother into a hug. He squeezed me tightly, but this time I had company in his arms. He'd pulled both Milo and Jack into the hug with me. Next to me, Milo smiled, but the squashed face of Jack next to him showed only an expression of pure terror.

"Unsquash Remy," I grinned and Remy let go.

"What now?" asked Milo.

"Now? I guess we read this book thoroughly and figure out exactly what to practice for the competition.

I woke early as the first light of dawn trickled sunlight through my curtains.

I'd spent hours practicing swordmanship with Milo in my room the night before and now my body ached. Muscles I didn't know I had burned, but if it meant I was getting better and Milo was getting better, I could survive a little pain. It had taken my mind off everything else going on. Things I couldn't control. The dragon situation, Morpheus, my upcoming wedding. I didn't want to think about any of it and so I didn't. I practiced sword fighting till I was too tired to do anything else.

No one had come to my room to drag him out so he'd stayed late, leaving me with a kiss way after dark. I jumped out of bed and opened the door expecting him not to be there, but he was. Dark circles blotched under his eyes, but when he saw me he broke into a delicious grin.

He moved forward and kissed me.

"My shift finished half an hour ago, but I didn't want to go without seeing you first."

"I'm surprised you are still working in this part of the castle."

"Me too," Milo said, lowering his voice. "but I stayed for my shift and no one complained. Well, Jack complained, but he always complains." He gave me a beautiful smile. "He left an hour ago."

He nodded his head towards another guard who had taken up a spot. This one was new. He was also mean looking and huge. My father really didn't want me to leave it seemed. When he caught me looking he gave me a leery grin.

"I have something to show you," I said to Milo, ignoring the other guard. "Do you think you'll be able to come see me later?"

"Show me now?" he asked, stifling a yawn.

I pulled him close and whispered in his ear, not wanting the other guard to hear. "You are tired. Go home and sleep. You need to be more awake to see this."

I'd deliberated all night about breaking my promise to Vasuki. I'd promised to tell my father about him and not tell anyone else. I'd failed miserably on the first part. My father didn't want to hear anything to do with Dragons. And here I was wanting to tell Milo about them. I needed to tell someone. I wasn't even going to tell him, I was going to show him.

He gave me a brief kiss goodbye and left. The other guard glared meanly so I shut the door, only to have it opened a few minutes later by Dahlia.

"You're dressed already," she said, noting the dress, I'd just pulled on.

"Always a tone of surprise," I said back to her.

"Well at least let me brush your hair," she said, bustling into my room. "I wouldn't want you putting me out of a job now." I stuck my tongue at her and sat on the chair, facing it out to the moorlands. It was too cloudy to see the peaks of the fire mountains, but I imagined the dragons were flying around as they always did.

"Have you ever heard of Morpheus?" I asked as she ran the brush through my hair, tugging the tangles out. I wasn't sure I could believe what Caspian had told me.

"He's one of the gods...God of sleep, I think," she mused aloud. "I don't know. There are so many of them. I don't know how people keep up with who they are worshiping these days."

"Don't you believe in the gods, Dahlia?" She'd never mentioned them, and I'd always took her as a non-believer like I was.

"It's all stuff and nonsense if you ask me. How can there be so many gods? It doesn't make sense. People believe what they want to believe. They believe whatever suits them."

"That's what I thought, too, but..."

"But?"

"Caspian was talking to me about a world run by a god named Morpheus, and I'd never heard of him before."

Dahlia tutted. "Well, the fae are a law unto themselves. They follow their own rules. I have to say, I'm glad that you are not being forced to marry him anymore. I don't like him much. "

"You've changed your tune," I said, remembering how she'd practically drooled over him last time he was mentioned. "Why not?"

"I've heard rumors that he's not nice to the staff. I know I'm not supposed to talk ill of your parents' guests, but I'm not sure either of them knows him like they think they do. Yes, he's utterly gorgeous, but that doesn't account for much now, does it?"

I gave her a wry grin

Dahlia thought the same of him as I did now that she'd finally seen past his pretty exterior. It was nice to have her on my side, even if she was practically yanking my hair out as she talked about him.

"Do you think Milo has a hope of winning against Caspian...in the competition I mean?" I assumed she already knew. Very little escaped Dahlia when it came to matters in the castle.

"I don't know. I've not seen either of them fight," She said, gathering my hair up and beginning a braid. "They've got quite a bit of competition too, so who knows really."

My ears pricked up. "Competition? What do you mean?"

"You don't think it's only them interested, do you? Once the story broke of the competition, every man in the land wanted in."

"What?" I asked queasily as she wrapped a ribbon around the end of the braid.

"Yes," she answered cheerfully, unaware of the nausea rising in my stomach. "Your father has been fielding inquiries all day. I don't think he's very happy about it. He's passed it to the castle admin staff to deal with, but they are swamped too."

"Other people want to marry me?" I gulped.

She moved around to get a look at my hair from the front. "Oh, yes. There's a line a mile long outside the castle wanting to join in."

"No!" I stood up and wandered to the window. As she had said, a line of men stretched as far as the eye could see. One of them saw me and pointed up to the window. Suddenly, I had the eyes of hundreds of men looking my way. I shut my curtains quickly.

"This was only supposed to be for Milo and Caspian," I croaked.

"Yes, well, if you open a can of worms, you have to be ready for the birds."

I sat back in my chair, feeling faint. I'd had enough on my

plate juggling two men that I didn't want to marry; now, I had a whole army of them.

"Why would anyone want to marry me?" I squeaked.

"You're a beautiful young lady, Azia. Why wouldn't they?"

"No one looked twice at me a couple of weeks ago," I argued.

Dahlia went to my bed and began to pull the covers straight. "I'm not sure that's true. You've always had your admirers. My son often asked about you when I went home. He's always had a crush on you."

"He has?"

"Yes. He was first in line to join the competition this morning. I told him he was a fool, but he wouldn't listen. I just hope your father doesn't come up with something too awful for it. I wouldn't want him getting hurt."

This wasn't supposed to happen," I complained. "I don't even want to get married. I'm only eighteen years old. I want to travel and see things. I want to know what it's like to be me before I know what it's like to be a part of someone else.

"I was married with a child on the way at your age," she said, plumping my pillows. I didn't have the opportunities you have. You are a princess. Just because you are married, doesn't mean you can't experience life. It just means you'll share those experiences with someone else. Besides, rumors about that fae chap of yours aren't the only ones going around the castle. I've heard that you are getting very close to that young guard."

I felt the blush rise to my cheeks. So the castle staff were talking about me. Didn't they have enough to talk about?

"I really like Milo, but he knows I don't want to get married so young. He's only doing this competition so I don't have to marry Caspian."

She put the last of my pillows back and placed her hands on her hips. "You have a great opportunity here. You have the best men in all the land lined up outside wanting to marry you, not to mention two in the castle."

"But most of them will only want what comes with the position," I sighed. "The castle, power, money."

"True," she nodded, "but the bravest will win."

"No, the best fighter will win, but will that necessarily be the best husband?"

"No, I guess not," she agreed, picking up a duster and beginning to dust. "Maybe your father will come up with a fair competition. I know he's under a lot of stress at the moment, and he's making some poor decisions, but I really do believe he has your best interests at heart. He will make it fair, and you never know, you might find the love of your life in all of this."

"I doubt it," I sighed, sitting back in the chair. I could no more imagine finding the love of my life than sprouting an extra head and turning green. "How is my father anyway? This must be an awful nuisance for him."

Dahlia pursed her lips. "You could say that. He's not happy at all that you've brought this on him. He has enough on his plate as it is with your mother being cursed and the dragon problem to deal with. I'd stay out of his way for a few days if I were you. I don't think you are his favorite person at the moment. "

My heart already ached with everything I had to deal with, and now, I'd hurt my father.

"That will be easy," I sighed. "I'm confined to my room. I can't leave even if I want to."

"Actually, that's not quite the case," Dahlia smiled. "That's why I'm here. I'm to make you look presentable."

"Presentable for what?"

"Your father wants you downstairs for a photoshoot with the Draconian Sentinel. Apparently, they've sent a photographer who is refusing to leave until he gets a photo and an interview."

"Why doesn't my father get the guards to throw him out? "I asked appalled.

"Because then the press will print a story that your father is under duress. Remember, he has a kingdom to run, and he's got to be a good leader while everything around him is falling apart. Let's just hope he's not going to stick around for the interview, eh?"

My stomach dropped at the thought of the mess I'd made. I couldn't see a way out any more than my father could, and now, it was going to be printed in the Draconis national newspaper.

Could anything worse happen?

Just then, there was a knock at the door. It opened without me moving to it.

"There you are!" Caspian walked in uninvited. "Your father asked me to escort you to the grand hall."

I looked at Dahlia. She shrugged her shoulders.

Just great! I stood up and walked past Caspian. There was no point pretending I cared anymore. As I passed, I slipped the ring box into his hand.

"I'm sorry," I whispered. I wasn't sure if he even heard me.

The great hall was in chaos, and any thoughts that my father might not be there were quashed. He looked so tired as he fielded questions from all over the place. There was no coordination, and it was difficult to tell who was who. I couldn't even see the photographer in amongst all the men.

Pushing through, I climbed the small stage to my father's throne.

I leaned down and whispered in his ear. "Go to bed. I've got this."

He shook his head, but he didn't move. His eyes were glazed over, the look of a man too exhausted to move.

"Gentlemen," I shouted to the rabble. When the noise didn't abate, I coughed then tried again, this time, shouting loudly.

"Gentlemen!"

This time a hundred pairs of eyes looked my way, and a light flashed. So the photographer was in there somewhere.

I'd given my first speech only a few days previously, but that was to the staff. This was my first time giving one to complete strangers, but with everything going on, it was about time I stepped up.

I cleared my throat and began to speak. "I appreciate you all coming here. It means a lot to me that you would all want to be considered to be my husband. I wasn't expecting such a turnout, but I am grateful to all of you. You are my father's loyal subjects, and therefore, you all mean a lot to me. Unfortunately, I am only one person, and I cannot marry you all."

A titter of laughter went around the hall as more men filtered in.

"As you probably already know, the kingdom is under a lot of strain at the moment, and it's not possible to see all of you today. Instead, I'd like all of you to write your name on a piece of paper along with your address to register your interest in the competition."

I motioned for one of the guards to fetch some pens and paper. "We will send you a personal invite a few days before the tournament, and we will print instructions in the Draconian Sentinel. Until then, I ask that you write your name quickly and leave us to come up with the rules of the competition. "

I asked the guard with the pens and paper to take them outside. They could line up there. One by one, they trooped out until there were only a few people left. A man with a notepad and one with a camera stayed behind.

"Dahlia," I said, my heart still thumping from having to

talk to so many people. "Please, will you help my father to his room while I give an interview for the Sentinel?"

My father rose. "I don't need any help. If you'll excuse me, gentlemen, it's been a long day."

Dahlia followed him anyway. Only Caspian remained.

"Is your father sick?" The reporter asked. He was already writing something in his pad. "He said it's been a long day, but it's still early morning."

"My father is perfectly well. He's just got a lot going on, as you can imagine. However, we are not here to talk about my father, we are here to discuss the competition. It will be held the week before the wedding. I have no information on what the competition will entail at this time, but the winning suitor will be the one to marry me."

"What if you don't like the winner?"

What if, indeed. "Then I shall marry him anyway as the law states. The competition will weed out anyone not suitable to the life of the queen's court. He will never be king. When I ascend to the throne, he will work alongside me, but will never be my equal, nor will he ever be above me in position. Not many men would like to be in such a position, so a word of warning to all the men that enter. This will be the life you will live, always second. I have no more answers, so if you'll please excuse me, gentlemen."

I walked past them with my head held high, ignoring the stares from the reporter and his photographer. That should cut down on idiots thinking they would be able to rule the kingdom by marrying me.

The castle was quiet as I walked back up to my room. When I got there, Milo stood outside. Without stopping, I grabbed his hand and pulled him down the corridor.

"Come with me."

"Where are we going?" he whispered as I spirited him through the castle. My father was asleep, and my mother cursed. I was the eldest child, and, therefore, the person in charge, but that didn't mean I wanted to be stopped by any member of staff brave enough to question where I was going. The big mean guard was absent this morning, but that didn't mean that there wouldn't be others like him.

Despite what my father said he wanted, I wasn't planning on spending the last remaining free days of my life locked in my room as though I'd done something wrong. I cared about this kingdom, and I needed to do something to help—anything. I didn't even know what, but I wasn't going to help anyone by sitting on my bed moping.

I took us out of the back entrance to the castle and across the grounds to the little door through the back wall. A thick brass lock held it tight to the frame.

"Now what?" Milo asked.

I turned to him and kissed him quickly on the nose, before expertly climbing up his body. He soon got the idea, clasping his hands together to give me a leg up the wall. When I was at the top, I leaned down to help him over.

"Are we going to practice?" he asked as we walked quickly through the small wooded area.

"No. The time for practice is over. It's now time to start doing."

We emerged into the sunshine at the base of the Fire Mountains.

"Doing what?"

I took his hand and began to lead him to the part of the wall I'd walked around last time. My father's army hadn't managed to build any more of it, and like everything else in Draconis at the moment, it had ground to a standstill. "I don't know yet," I replied cryptically, "but I know someone who might."

We climbed a little way before I felt comfortable enough to use my magic. I'd kept this part of myself away from Milo, afraid that he might think there was something wrong with me, but I couldn't keep it in any longer. I was magic, and even though I wasn't sure exactly how to use it, I knew it was worth figuring it out. Maybe one day I'd be able to help my mother. It only ever seemed to work when I was close to the dragons, but that was fine as I could already see a couple of them flying high above us.

"Watch this!" I said, before pulling my hand from Milo's and closing my eyes.

I concentrated for all I was worth, pulling all my energy to a central point deep in my belly before letting it blast out of my hands and spiraling up into the cloudless sky.

The people would have been able to see it. Even as far away as Zhore, but it didn't matter. As long as the Dragons saw it first.

"Azia?" Milo asked, grabbing my sleeve. I ignored him as best I could, even after the pulling on my sleeve became all the more insistent.

"Azia!" He was louder now, but I was in the zone. When he tugged me so hard, we both collapsed to the ground, the beam of magical light disappeared.

It happened so quickly. Milo jumped to his feet and pulled out his sword, ready for a fight. My heart raced for a second before realizing who it was he was up against. A flash of purple in the corner of my eye told me my friend was here. I pulled myself up next to Milo, and this time, it was my turn to pull on his sleeve. "Put your sword away. That's Nyre. That's who I brought you here to see."

Milo turned to me, a look of disbelief on his face, but he didn't lower his sword. "You brought me to see a dragon? Are you serious?"

I nodded, then waved at Nyre, who landed next to us as Milo watched on with mild concern. He didn't sheath his sword as Nyre skipped towards us and flew up onto my shoulder like she had before.

"Woah!" I held my hands out at Milo, who'd readied himself for attack, his sword aloft and his mouth a perfect o shape. "She's a friend. Milo, this is Nyre, Nyre this is Milo. His bark's worse than his bite."

Milo gazed at me goggle-eyed as Nyre pranced on my shoulder, before hopping over to Milo's. He'd ducked, but not in time. Nyre had got him. She wanted a stage to dance on, and he was it. I laughed as she hopped up and down on his head playfully. When Milo saw he was in no danger, he relaxed. Nyre hopped back over to me as Milo put his sword away.

If he thought cute little Nyre was scary, wait until he met Vasuki and Emba and the other dragons. He was in for a shock, but I wasn't going to spill the beans.

"Do you think you can get one of the others to come fly us up the mountain?" I whispered in Nyre's ear. I didn't want Milo hearing. It would spoil the surprise.

She tightened the grip on my shoulder as she prepared to launch herself upward. Or at least, I thought that's what she was doing before I found myself flying up into the air with her. She swooped and grabbed Milo with her spare talon and began the ascent to her mountaintop home.

Color drained from Milo's face as we flew at a dizzying speed upward. He didn't say a word, and I think that was only because he would throw up if he dared to open his mouth

I thought we'd fly into the nest we'd flown into before, but Nyre carried on flying over the other side of the mountain to a valley I'd not seen before. A small river twisted through it flanked by huge houses dotting the scenery.

"Where is this place?" Milo whispered, his voice almost lost

on the wind. I had to strain to hear him, but I got the gist. I
had no answers for him. Dragons were everywhere. I didn't
know where we were. As we got closer, the houses became
more pronounced. Each of them was made in a haphazard
manner with what looked like found objects, and all of them
had two doors. One normal-sized and another huge door. My
mouth went dry as I noticed we weren't alone. The dragons in
the air had begun to follow us, and as we neared the ground,
the ones down there dropped whatever it was that they were
doing and followed suit. Behind me, Milo gripped me tightly
as we ended up the head of a parade of angry looking dragons.

I'd gone against my promise to Vasuki not to bring
another person here. On the other side of the mountain, it
had seemed like a good idea, but now that we were
surrounded, I was beginning to rethink my decision. Not
that I could do anything about it. We'd already landed. There
was no going back.

Milo pulled out his sword again the moment Nyre let go
of him.

I let my hand fall on his and softly lowered it. "They are
not a threat."

I hope.

One of the nearest dragons bared its teeth, saliva dripping
from its large jowls.

"Are you sure?" Milo hissed. "Because I'm beginning to
feel like dragon-breakfast."

Gazing around at the dozens of eyes watching me, I
began to wonder if I hadn't overestimated my welcome here.

Inside me, my body responded to the dragons the way it
had when I'd been out with Caspian. My magic or whatever
it was began to stir. I'd spent so many hours trying to
recreate it with no success, but now, it was churning, boiling
away inside me. I threw it out, sending a beacon up into the
sky. This time rains of hot pink and purple fell like cherry

blossoms in spring. As they had before, the dragons dropped to their bellies, bowing down to me.

Milo gripped my hand tightly as the whole village of dragons came thundering down.

Between them walked a man and woman, if you could call them that. I bowed my head as Vasuki and Emba walked hand in hand through the crowd of dragons.

"What's this?" Vasuki asked, eyeing Milo.

My stomach had been in knots, but Vasuki didn't appear to be angry, merely curious to the stranger beside me.

I held my breath as I introduced Milo.

Vasuki walked forward, his hand extended. Beside me, Milo hesitantly held out his own hand. To give him credit, he stood tall and firm, though I could see a small tremor in him. I should have warned him before, but I was afraid he might not come if I did.

"My father wouldn't listen to me," I said as Emba pulled Milo into a hug. "I tried, but he is under a lot of strain, and he thinks I'm causing trouble. I've told no one else. Milo didn't even know until I brought him here. He is the only one who listens to me. I'm sorry if I have gone against your wishes."

I bowed my head to him.

Behind him, someone growled. It was the green dragon from earlier, but now, he was transformed into a grizzly beast of a man. With his green hair and scaled skin, he looked more moss than man. He also did not look impressed.

"Darius, know your place," Vasuki growled back, and the man took a step back. "This is our queen, and this is her guest. Respect her as such."

Darius growled again and stalked away, disappearing into a nearby house.

"Queen?" Milo whispered, arching his brow. "Do you want to, at least, give me a hint at what's going on here?"

"Remember when you called me Queen of the Dragons?"

He nodded.

"Well, it turned out you were right...sort of."

Turning back to Vasuki, I bowed again.

"I come to ask your guidance. I have no one to help me, and there are people I'm not sure I can trust. I do trust you, however, and I'd value your honesty."

"I am nothing if not honest. Bluntly so, at times. How can I help you?"

"I've have been told of a place called the Dream Realm. I wonder if you know of it?"

"I have heard of such a place," he confirmed. "We do not worship gods in the way that you humans do. There is no dragon god. We believe that we are the higher beings. That doesn't mean I do not know of them. However, I am not the best person to ask of such a place. You must know people better than I who can tell you about it. What about that fae I saw you with the other day. If anyone knows about the gods, it is he."

"He was the one who told me about the Dream Realm, but he is the one I can't trust. I fear I'll have to travel to find someone who knows. I am sorry for taking up your time."

"I already told you that you are welcome up here any time that you desire. Your friend here also, but only with you. I request that you don't bring anyone else up here. I have been more than fair with you even though you went against my wishes. There is only so much I can do to keep you safe. You saw how Darius reacted to your presence. I am not his keeper, and there is only so much he will take."

"I understand. I promise I will not tell another soul about you, although, as you requested before, I will try and get through to my father. He is having a difficult time. He still wants to send his men to the mountaintops to kill you all. I've not had a chance to talk him out of it. I don't think he really wants to hurt any of you, but the people are looking to him to take action, and he is a broken man. He knows not what he is doing now since my mother fell asleep."

"I understand. Things must be hard, and I do not envy him. I will keep this information away from Darius, but I'd like you to do me one more favor. "

I nodded enthusiastically. I owed him as much.

"Can you send a beacon of light up as a warning if you see anyone climbing the mountains? It will give us time to prepare. I will make my people safe by hiding them rather than fighting back, but the women nest on the mountaintops and are the most vulnerable. I do not want a war with your father. I will extend this as a courtesy to you for the time being. Is there anything else I can help you with, my queen?"

I was about to say no, but then Derillen popped into my mind. "You were around eighteen years ago. I've asked my family and my servant about my history and about that of my mother. I only get half-truths. Do you know where I came from?"

He shook his head. "I have told you before that I do not pay attention to what happens down in the human world. There was a shift of magic at around that time. It has shifted again recently. We are heading for dark times. My magic only extends to the changing of my shape. I am no fae and no magician."

"My magic only works at certain times too."

"Ah, now that, I can tell you about. I do not understand why. It is clear that you are not a dragon shifter with us, but your magic has elevated you to your position. I believe it is the magic of the dragons, and therefore, only works when we are around. I feel your great power, but I believe it is limited. We are naturally drawn to you and the light that comes from you. No other person has been able to do that, but that does not mean you will be able to do anything else. Of course, I could be wrong. "

He hesitated for a second. "Actually, there are other magic users in Draconis that might help you to understand your powers. It's a long shot. They are as mistrusting of humans as we are, but they have their own brand of magic."

"Who?"

"The dwarves," Milo answered for him.

"You are correct. They live beneath us in the depths of the mountains. We do not like to mix with them, but we have a mutual arrangement. We protect them from humans up here, and they provide us with gold. It is a mutually beneficial agreement, but that is all. We do not socialize, and I cannot promise you will find what you are looking for."

"Thank you." I didn't hold out much hope that the dwarves would be able to help us, but I had no other leads to go on, and as Vasuki said, they were magic users.

"If that is all, I will take you back down the mountain. Night is drawing near.."

It was indeed getting darker.

He shifted quickly, allowing Milo and I to jump on his back, which was a marked difference to the way Nyre flew us. Less terrifying for a start. He dropped us off near the base of the mountain, leaving us to walk the last part.

We'd not learned much, but at least, Milo finally knew my secret. A secret I'd hated keeping to myself.

In the woods, he stopped me.

"What?"

He cleared his throat. "I can probably get us in to see the dwarves. Humans generally aren't allowed in their mine, but they know me. It's possible that they will talk to you. I don't know what they can tell you, though. They don't care about human gods any more than the dragons do."

I sat on the boulder we'd used to drop our armor on before and dropped my head to my hands.

"I don't know what else to do, Milo. I have my father

trying to get me married and hundreds of men wanting to marry me. My mother is sick, and no one believes me that it's Derillen. They all think it's some copycat, but I know it's her, and I know she wants me. I've been told lies about my history all my life, and I don't know who I can trust anymore."

I felt the tears begin to sting my eyes.

He pulled my face up so I was looking right at him.

"You can trust me. I don't know anything about Derillen, and I can't do anything for the queen, but I'm going to enter that competition, and I'm going to win."

I nodded my head slowly.

"And until then, I'll be right by your side while we try and figure out what is going on."

He kissed my cheeks, wetting his lips with my tears.

He spoke with such earnestness, but how could he compete with over a hundred men? I was going to end up married to a total stranger.

"If you are going to beat this thing," I said, my voice wavering. "We will need to practice." I pulled my sword out and stood up. With a smile, he did the same, matching my stance.

We had no armor with us, so we couldn't try too hard without the risk of hurting each other. I didn't even know if sword fighting was one of the things my father would add to the competition, but if it was, I needed Milo to be the best.

We spent hours like that, just the two of us with our swords and our freedom. When it became so dark, we could no longer continue, so we walked back into the castle. I half-expected my father to be waiting for me, but he wasn't. I kissed Milo quickly outside my bedroom door and shut it behind me.

"You've been out a while."

My heart lurched, and my breath caught in my throat. In front of me, the bolt on the door closed of its own accord.

Turning, I found Caspian lying on my bed, a smug grin on his face.

"I thought we'd established that you were not to come into my room without permission," I said, storming over to him.

"I remember, but I thought you'd want to know. I've found out how to get into the Dream Realm."

*B*reakfast was a miserable affair with both my mother and father missing. Ash and Hollis had wolfed down their food and had left, leaving only Remy and me.

He sat gazing at his bowl, an empty stare down at the food he'd not touched. That wasn't like him at all. Remy loved food, and yet, he'd not even picked up his spoon.

"You okay, Remy?"

He looked up, dazed as though he'd forgotten I was even there.

When he spoke, his voice came out in a whisper. "Mama."

My heart dropped. He missed our mother. Of course, he did. The castle was in chaos, and Remy didn't understand what was going on. I'd been so preoccupied with my own problems that I'd not thought about Remy. Standing up, I rounded the table and brought him into a hug.

"It's going to be alright, Remy. Mama is asleep. Would you like me to take you to see her?"

He nodded his head, and a little of his sparkle came back. Had no one thought to take him to see her in all this time? It broke my heart to think how confusing all this would be for him.

"Can you eat your breakfast first? Momma likes to know you've been eating properly."

He obediently picked up his spoon and began to spoon the cereal into his mouth, bringing a small smile to my face. I made a mental note to pay more attention to him. He had his own member of staff just as I did, but she was only to help him get dressed and bathe and get to bed. Unlike myself and my other brothers, it had been my mother who had taken most of the responsibility for Remy. There'd barely been a minute in his whole life that he hadn't had her at his side, and now, he'd gone over a week without her.

"Come on, honey," I said once his cereal was finished. Taking his hand, I led him up to our mother's room. Knocking quietly, I opened the door. I expected my father to be there, but it was only my mother's maid. She dropped a book she'd been reading onto my mother's nightstand and looked towards us guiltily.

"It's ok," I said. "I don't mind you reading. We are here for a visit."

"Very well, Your Highness." She stood and curtseyed.

"How is she?" I asked, although it was obvious. There was no change in my mother. She slept as soundly as she had the last time I saw her.

The maid stood, picking her book up and lowered her eyes. "Still the same, I'm afraid. I've been moving her position to prevent bedsores, but I'm not sure there is anything else I can do for her. I wish there was."

I nodded my head. "That's fine. Thank you."

The maid walked past us, leaving just Remy and me in the room with our sleeping mother. She looked like an angel in sleep. Her perfect face rested peacefully. I hoped that wherever she was, whichever part of the Dream Realm she was in, it was a nice place. Caspian hadn't mentioned much about what it was like except to say that her exits were blocked.

"Mama," Remy said, approaching her cautiously. He stroked her face the way I'd seen her do to him a thousand times.

"She's asleep, Remy," I told him. "She worked so hard looking after us and being the queen that she needs a lot of rest."

He looked at me and nodded. I wasn't sure if he really understood. It was hard to tell with Remy, but I could see the grief in his eyes. He pulled the covers back quickly. My heart started to race as I wondered what he was going to do. He climbed in next to her and snuggled up next to her body, closing his own eyes.

"Are you tired, Remy?" Had he even been sleeping himself, or had he lain awake as I had, worrying about everything? I had no way of knowing, but he looked so sweet and comfortable snuggled up to her that I didn't have the heart to move him. I wondered if somewhere my mother could feel him beside her. I hoped so. I hoped it would bring them both comfort. I pulled the cover back over both of them and kissed Remy's cheek. A small smile came to his lips.

"I'll let you nap here and come back for you later, okay?"

He nodded his head almost imperceptively and closed his eyes.

I left him there, feeling a little bit better about having ignored him for the past week and headed through the castle to somewhere I never expected I'd ever voluntarily go. I went to Caspian's room.

After throwing him out of my own room last night without hearing him out, I figured I probably should go and find out what he had to say. If there was any way of getting my mother out of the curse she was in, I'd do anything, even if it meant listening to Caspian.

"Hello," he said, opening his door with the same smug grin on his face he'd been wearing the night before. "I knew you'd come to me, eventually."

I bit back the vomit rising in my throat and gave him a smile of my own. It wasn't one of pleasure.

"Shut it, buster. I'm here to find out how I can save my mother, and that's all."

He tapped his fingers against the doorframe. "You didn't seem to care last night when you were unceremoniously throwing out me out of your room."

"I was tired, and I was angry because of you," I said, my anger rising. Every conversation I had with this guy made my blood boil. I took a deep breath and plastered on a smile. "I've calmed down now, so if you'd please let me know."

He wavered. "It's a pity..."

I sighed. "What's a pity?"

"I thought you were here for something else," he said, raising an inquiring eyebrow. "I thought you wanted my company." His smug grin widened.

Sanctimonious bastard!

"I'm not sure how I can say this without offending you, but seeing as I don't care about your feelings, I'm going to go right ahead and say it anyway. I do not want your company. I've never wanted your company, and I see no reason why I would ever want your company."

"Well, then," he said, his hand dropping from the door-frame to the door handle. "I see no reason why I should tell you what I know."

I pulled out my sword and held it to his throat.

"Is this reason enough?" I said. This time, the smug grin was all mine.

He held his hands up and backed into the room.

"Tell me what you know," I growled.

Quick as a whip, his sword matched mine, knocking it away from his face.

His grin returned, but I'd been practicing with Milo and was better than I'd ever been. He seemed surprised as I came back from his defense, recovering quickly.

His eyebrows rose, but the grin remained. "I see you've bettered yourself. What fun. I do like an opponent who can fight back."

Every thrust I gave, he parried. We were now equally matched. "We both know you can't kill me," I said, sweat forming on my brow as the exertion of keeping up with him was beginning to wear me down. He was good, really good, and I wasn't better than him. Not yet, but I would be.

"We do, do we? I don't recall signing anything," he said.

"Sign this!" I shouted out, slicing through the top layer of his immaculate jacket. He looked down at the rip, surprise filling his eyes.

Now, he really came at me, and it took every bit of effort I had not to fail under the pressure. It was like fighting a whirlwind, and everywhere my sword was, his was there ready to knock it down.

I panted, as the fight became something it was never meant to be. Dangerous. I'd only meant to scare him, not to injure, but I could see by the look in his eyes, that we were both beyond that point. This was a fight to the death.

Dragon balls, my father was going to kill me himself if Caspian didn't. What a ridiculous position to find myself in.

"I surrender!" I said, pulling back and narrowly missing the sharp end of his sword. Almost instantaneously, I found myself lying flat on my back on his bed, him lying on top of me. His hot breath came quickly, a sign that he was as exhausted by our fight as I was.

"Get. off. me!" I growled, shoving him in the belly with my hand. Unfortunately, my sword was in my other hand.

"I don't know," he mused. "Why should I?"

He had a point. He had me completely at his mercy, and I was in no position to make demands. Damn it all!

"Because if you don't, I'll slice your head off so quickly you'll be looking at your back from the wrong angle."

Caspian craned his head around to see who was speaking, and I looked over his shoulder to see Milo standing in the doorway, his sword held aloft.

The weight on me lessened as Caspian stood up, his hands in the air.

"Just a little fun and games," he said. I sat up and gulped down a couple of breaths.

"Actually, Caspian was going to tell me how I can find my mother. He says he knows how to get into the Dream Realm."

"I suggest you talk then," Milo said, cocking his head to the side to indicate the bed. He pressed his sword to Caspian's chest to give him no option but to sit back on the bed. I jumped out of the way as he sat down.

A sneer came over Caspian's face. "I could defeat you with magic right now. I don't even need to pick up my sword to fight you."

It was true. The first time he'd come into my room, he'd made my old sword disappear with a wave of his wand.

I stood up in front of him and considered being nice to him, then I decided against it. "Look, Caspian. You've come here as a guest of my father. I don't think he will take too lightly to you fighting his guards, not to mention his only daughter. One word to him, and he'll have you packing your bags. I suggest that if you want to stay here and still be included in the competition to win my hand in marriage, you tell me what you know."

He seemed to consider my words. I had no clue why the guy would want to marry me. He clearly couldn't stand me.

Perhaps, it was about power. Whatever it was, he backed down.

"There is only one way into the Dream Realm from the outside without dreaming, but you will not find it in this kingdom. It is not in a set place, so it is hard to find. Only the Morpheus himself can open the portal."

"So how do we find it?" I asked, biting back a curse. I was getting more and more frustrated by the second.

Caspian shrugged, the grin creeping back onto his face. "That's where your problem lies. You need to find Morpheus."

"How?" Milo asked.

Caspian shrugged. "I don't know. He's a god. He lives in a place that we mere mortals cannot get to. Only in death do we travel there."

I sucked in a deep breath and tried hard to refrain from hitting him square in the nose. He was enjoying this a little too much.

"So you are telling me that to save my mother from dying, I have to die first in order to enter the portal to the Dream Realm and then come back to life once I return from it?

"No," he replied. "Once you are dead, you are dead. There is no coming back. The dead are not able to enter the Dream Realm at all. Dead people don't dream."

I stood, frustration running through me. "Let's go," I said to Milo. "This guy is wasting our time."

"You could, however, try and find him when he is in our realm. The mortal realm. Maybe if he is feeling generous, he might let you into his domain."

"How do you even know this? You said you'd ask your friend."

"And, so I did," he answered.

"You told me your friend lives in Urbis. That's three days' journey on the Urbis Express or longer by train."

"I have many ways to contact my friends, none of which I wish to share with you. Why do you care anyway as long as you get the information?"

I did care because it was awfully convenient that he had "ways" to speak to his friend, who was days away. It didn't lend much credibility to his story.

I walked toward the door.

"You won't find him anyway," Caspian continued. "It's extremely rare that the gods come down to the mortal realm. It's not unheard of, but it's rare. Even then, you could speak to him directly and not even know it's him. The gods don't like to make their presence known. They are masters of disguise. You could look for him forever, and never find him."

He was still giggling as I slammed the door shut behind me.

"What a jerk!" Milo said.

"Do you think he was lying?" I asked. I wanted Morpheus to be real, just so there was something I could do. Some way of bringing my mother back. I was willing to latch onto anything, even if it came from that lying scumbag.

Milo shrugged. "I don't know. I never held much stock with Gods and religion."

"I guess there's one way to find out."

I strode down the corridor so quickly that Milo had to run to keep up with me. "Hey, where are you going?"

"I'm going to my room to pack. I can't stay here anymore. You heard him. I have to find Morpheus. If there's a chance that Caspian is telling the truth, I need to know."

"Yeah, I heard him. I also heard when he said it would be impossible to find him. What about the competition?"

I turned to face him. "I don't want anything to do with the stupid competition. You know that. I never did. I don't want to get married. Not even to you."

I saw his face drop a little, and I realized how harsh I sounded.

"I'm sorry. You've become so important to me these past couple of weeks. I like you a lot. I can't imagine a life where you are not in it and one day, yes I'd like to get married. I can see a beautiful wedding surrounded by our friends and family. Your mother will create a lovely tiara for me, and my parents will be there looking on proudly. I can see your face full of love, and I can feel the happiness in my heart. But none of that will happen if I get married in a couple of weeks when my father wants me to. Marriage to you would fill me with joy, but not like this. Not because I have to. We don't even know each other. We've been dating for less than two weeks, and most of that was fake dating. There's every chance you won't win anyway. There are so many entries. Who knows what will happen?"

"I love you," he said, breaking my heart into pieces.

Tears coursed down my face. I leaned forward and kissed him slowly. It would have to be enough. He had loved me for a long time. I'd only just met him.

He held my hand. "You don't have to spend your life looking for Morpheus, you know. There is another way."

I smiled, grateful for the change in subject. I wasn't ready for declarations of love. I wasn't ready for any of it.

"We only have to find Derillen," he explained. "She is the one stopping your mother from leaving the Dream Realm, according to Caspian, right?"

I sighed. "Yes, but she could be anywhere. Where would I even start?"

Milo took my hand. "Where would we start? I'm coming with you. At least, you know what she looks like. With Morpheus, we don't even know that."

I nodded. What he said made sense. "Where do we start?"

"I guess we start where your dragon friends told us to. We start in the mines."

I wiped my tears on the back of my sleeve. Had my mother been around, she would have told me off, but she wasn't around. We walked back through the castle, hand in hand. I didn't know what I could do, but I was determined to do something. My father collared us as we entered the long corridor that led to my room. Nerves took over as I realized I'd gone against his wishes...Again.

"There you are. I've been searching the castle for you. I thought I'd told you to stay in your room?"

"I'm sorry, Fath..."

He waved my words away. "Never mind about that now. I'm up to my eyeballs with stress over this competition you've gotten everyone into. No, don't apologize again. I've hardly been the exemplary father I should have been. Stress, you know. I'm the one who should be apologizing. A good night's sleep has done me a world of good. Anyway, I've looked through that book of yours, and the details of the competition are very vague. It seems to involve a lot of fighting. I was thinking of asking Caspian to sort it out, but then I realized that it would hardly be a fair fight if he's one of the competitors. My advisors are all busy, and I have had no time to do anything, so I want you to do it."

"You want me to plan the competition?"

Hope rose in my chest as I took in his words. If I was in charge of the competition, I could sway it in Milo's favor. I knew where his strengths and weaknesses lay, and he could help. I just wouldn't have to let my father know that.

"I'll do it."

From the corner of my eye, I saw Milo giving me a funny look. Only minutes before, I was ready to leave the castle before the competition took place.

"Wonderful," Father said, handing me a sheet of paper

covered in scribbles. "Here are some notes I made, but the rest will be up to you. You'll have to coordinate things with my secretary and the press. This needs to be finalized within the week if we have any hope for getting it sorted out in time. I think I'm going to have to ask you to plan the wedding too. I know it's a lot to ask. Caspian was going to do it, but it's a bit unfair to ask the chap to plan a wedding that might not be his."

"Thank you, Daddy," I said, giving him a kiss on the cheek. He was back to his old self. Lack of sleep and excessive stress had turned him into someone I no longer recognized, but the old king was back.

"I need to speak to you about the dragons," I said, glad that I'd finally caught him in a good mood. Vasuki and the others had been playing on my mind the whole time, but this was the first time I'd been able to get my father to listen to me.

"What about them?"

"I've met them." I held my breath as he took the information in.

"I'm aware. I saw one carrying you, remember."

And so he had. He'd fired arrows at Nyre. "Nyre is just one of the dragons I've met."

"Look," he said, holding up his hand to me. "I'm well aware you went up the mountain without my permission. I'm also aware that the dragons are shifters. Your grandfather told me before he died. Why do you think I started the wall? However, they still attacked my men."

"Not all of them," I argued. "It was just a few. They are angry."

"Well, they wouldn't be the only ones now, would they?"

"People have been going up the mountain to steal eggs. The leader, Vasuki, doesn't want to attack."

"I don't really wish to speak to you about this. Please don't take me for an idiot. I know a lot more than you think I do, but my loyalty is to my men, my people. They attacked us. I don't have all my knights back yet, but when they all return, I will be sending them up the mountain."

"But..."

"No more, Azia." He turned and walked away.

"It's a fight for another day," Milo said. "The knights might not be back for weeks. Draconis is a huge kingdom."

I nodded. He was right.

I thought you weren't interested in this competition.

"That was before I realized we could make it so you win. Yeah, I'd like to wait, but this way, at least, my father is happy, and I won't break his heart by running away."

"One other good thing has come of all this," said Milo taking my hand.

"Yeah?"

"Your father didn't send you back to your room. He seems to have forgotten that he grounded you for the rest of your life. We can go to the mines without having to sneak out the back way."

I gave him a grin, and the pair of us stole out of the castle. We did end up taking the back way, anyway, mainly because it was the quickest route.

"There are small doors all over the mountain," I said as we strolled through the woods.

"You don't want to use one of them," Milo replied. "They don't like humans, and they especially don't like humans going where they are not wanted. There is only one way you will get to speak to them, and that is by walking in through the front door."

"They have a front door?"

Milo laughed. "Yes. How do you think my father got in to work every day when he worked with them? He didn't climb the mountain. About three miles from here, there is a front door. Anyone can enter. It's basically a shop with a back entrance to the mines. The shop is where my father worked. He was the go-between for the dwarves and the humans. They didn't like to speak to us mere humans, so my father had to do it. It was a necessity for them, and they tolerated him. I think they even grew fond of him after a while. I was allowed in the shop sometimes. They know who I am. Whether they will listen to me or talk to me is another matter."

"Won't they talk to me?" I asked. "I'm the daughter of the king, after all."

"That means nothing to them. They don't have the same rules as we do, and they recognize no one as their king. Don't worry. I think I'll be able to get us an audience."

We came out of the woods. I blinked as the sun filtered into my eyes. Milo pointed out the road we would have to take. It was a little more than a track that skirted the base of the mountains. My father's men had gone back to work on the wall because it now stretched further than before.

"We won't be able to climb up to see the dragons for much longer," I pointed out as we began the trek that would take us to the mine entrance.

"You'll always be able to get up there, remember? Your friends will fly you up."

"I guess," I answered. "It seems an awfully long way to go. How did your father travel there every day from Zhore?"

"My father took a horse."

A horse! Why didn't I think of that? It would have made the journey a whole lot quicker. It was then, I remembered something better.

I pulled my magic into myself. It was useless in any other way, but it was great for getting dragons to come to me. I was getting better at it too. I thought of Nyre only. There was no point bringing the others down here. Vasuki had been kind to me so far, but I doubted his patience would last if I asked him to carry me places. Nyre was small, but she'd already heaved Milo and me up the mountain. She would bridge that eight miles in no time. Plus, she was so eager to help. A small jet of light escaped my hands, shooting up into the sky. A small dot appeared circling it, getting lower and lower until the purple scales of Nyre's armor became more apparent.

"We are traveling by dragon?"

I shrugged. "Why not? My father has use of all the horses, and I'm yet to get one of my own. This way, I won't have to bother anyone."

"Anyone, but your friend!" Milo tipped his eyes to the pretty young dragon that landed next to us.

"Nyre, would you mind taking us to the entrance of the Dwarf mines?"

Nyre jumped up and down in excitement. I nodded towards Milo to come to me. This time, I held his hand as we were hoisted up into the air. It would have been better if she was big enough to have us sit on her back, but she was still too small for that. Maybe I should have called for Vasuki or one of the bigger dragons, after all, I thought as my fingers turned white from being gripped so hard.

"I guess I shouldn't put anything to do with heights in the competition," I said, laughing at Milo's expression. His eyes were firmly clamped shut.

Nyre landed us on the ground with a soft bump. Milo sucked in a couple of deep breaths, and his face gained back the color that had drained from it when we were flying.

Once she saw we were fine, she once again took off into the sky. I watched her for a few seconds as she circled around up high.

"I think she'll wait for us," I said to Milo.

The entrance was nothing like I expected. I'd expected

another door like the little wooden doors I'd seen dotted around the mountains. Or maybe a huge wooden door with a keep out sign on it and lots of bolts. As it was, it looked like any other shop, with windows full of metal objects. Armour and jewelry sparkled in the midday sun. Yes, it was like any other shop, but it was built right into the very base of the mountains. A sign above the entrance chiseled right into the rock, said Mine Shop.

"They don't actually make all this stuff," Milo explained as we walked through the entrance. "A lot of this was made by my mother. That sword over there is one of mine." He pointed out a sword. It was gorgeous, but nothing as grand as the dragon sword he made for me.

"They paid us extra to work with their metal for the storefront. All they do is supply the metals and gems. The people who buy it get to do what they want with the metal once it's bought. The dwarves don't really understand things like jewelry or swords, but they do know it's what the people want. They are simple folk. They mine the metal, imbue it with magic, and get food in exchange."

"People buy metal with food?"

"Yes. The dwarves don't want money. They don't like to leave their home, so they wouldn't be able to spend it. Besides, they literally have gold. What they don't have is a means to feed themselves. They cannot forage or garden. They hate being out in the sunlight. So they sell their metal in exchange for food or whatever else it is they might need. Sometimes, they will accept cloth for clothes. Don't be fooled that they are getting the raw end of the bargain. They know how much their stuff is worth, and they price accordingly. An ounce of gold can cost a whole cow. One imbued with a certain magic can cost upwards of a whole herd of cows. They are famous and get people from all over all the kingdoms not just ours."

Inside, the shop was dark, and nothing like the modern outside would have led me to believe. If anything, this is how I expected the place to look, with roughly hewn walls and an air of dampness. The smell of sulfur permeated the air. I wrinkled my nose and checked out the shop. Along one wall was a glass counter with ingots of different precious metals in it. Behind the counter, a tall reedy man stood. He was talking to another man in a hood. They were haggling over the price of something.

"I'll give you a goat for it," the shorter man said, pointing to one of the smaller ingots.

The tall one shook his head impatiently and clucked. "You know I cannot accept that. The dwarves would fire me on the spot if they thought I was giving away their metal."

The smaller of the two sighed. "How about two goats and you throw in a couple of gems?"

"Hmm. How about two goats, we forget the gems, and I give you a smaller ingot?"

"Fine," the smaller man grumbled. "I'll take the ingot and bring the goats back tomorrow."

The tall man raised an eyebrow.

"Okay, okay, I'll come back with the goats first." The man shuffled past us, his face a look of pure misery.

"Still the hard-ass, I see," Milo said. The man's expression softened immediately.

"Milo. Good to see you." He held out his hand to Milo's. "You are not here to take my job, are you, because I happen to know the Dwarves will have you back in a heartbeat."

"Not this time, Lou. I'm actually here to introduce my friend to the dwarves."

Lou held his hands up. "You know I can't do that. They don't speak to..." He stopped as soon as his eyes landed on me. Half a second later, he fell into a bow.

"I'm sorry, Your Highness, I didn't recognize you for a moment. Please forgive my impudence."

I bit back a grin.

"It's fine. I only come here in need of your help."

Lou stood tall and rubbed his hands together. "I would love to help you. Unfortunately, I know for certain that the dwarves will not let you in. They bow down to no one and recognize no royalty the way we do. I'm most awfully sorry. If there was anything I could do, I would," he said apologetically.

"Tell the dwarves that we think the princess is somehow connected to the change in magic," Milo said. "We are not here just for our own benefit, but for that of everyone."

Lou wavered. "I'm not sure I can do anything."

"Come on, Lou. You know as well as I do that the dwarves will be feeling the magical vibrations. I can't feel it, but I've heard from enough sources to know that there has been a massive shift in magical energy."

"Well, they have been talking," Lou said uncomfortably. "I don't really like to listen in to be honest,though."

"Is Goethe here? Can you tell him Milo wants to talk to him?" Milo turned to me. "Goethe is the one dwarf that I've met. He's the one who asked me to stay on when my father died. He owes me."

Lou sighed, then walked past us and changed the Open sign to Closed on the door. I'll go fetch him, but don't expect him to be happy about it. He's been in a grump for the last two weeks."

"How can you tell?" Milo laughed. "He's always in a grump."

"Yes, well, he's worse than usual. Take a seat, and I'll go ask him if he wants to see you. I wouldn't hold your breath, though. Sorry Your Highness," he said again, looking my way and giving a little bow as he left through a tunnel at the back of the shop.

"Do you think this Goethe will be mad?" I asked.

Milo took my hand and gave it a squeeze. "Probably, but I wouldn't worry. He's always mad. It's his go-to response to everything. He's a big baby, really. Don't let his grouchiness fool you."

"Hmm." I sat back and twiddled my thumbs. Seconds later, a small man with more wrinkles than a prune and way too much skin waddled out.

"What?" he barked at Milo. "I thought we'd finally got rid of you."

Milo stood and walked over to the dwarf. "Not a chance, old man. I'm actually here for your help."

"So I hear," he grumbled. "Although, I don't know what you think I can do to help."

"We think you know something about the change in magical energy."

"So?"

"So, my friend Azia would like to know what you know. She thinks her family might be involved in some way. Her mother was the woman who was cursed."

Goethe turned his face to me. "The queen is cursed again? I should have known. You two had better come with me."

Lou's mouth dropped open as we trooped past him into the dark tunnel.

The stench of sulfur intensified as we walked into the gloom, and this time, it was my turn to be nervous.

"I've never once been let down here," Milo whispered. "My father was not allowed either. This thing must be huge if they are letting humans in."

"I'm not letting humans in; I'm letting you two in. That's different." Goethe barked.

I giggled until I remembered Vasuki's words. You are not

human. I'd pushed them to one side, marking them as ridiculous. Of course, I was human, but did Goethe think the same thing? I'd not mentioned to Milo that particular part of the conversation. Maybe it was just the way he'd said it. Milo was human, after all.

The smell of sulfur intensified, the deeper we walked into the mountain, and the temperature climbed.

My sense of unease along with it.

"Is it safe?" I whispered, trying to keep my volume below that which Goethe could hear.

I was not successful.

"Yes, it's safe. I don't eat humans on Tuesdays," he barked back.

I looked at Milo, who grinned and shrugged his shoulders.

"Today is Monday!" I mouthed

Ahead of us loomed a huge room filled with bright flames, which probably accounted for the soaring temperature. How Goethe and the other dwarves managed to work in such temperatures was beyond belief. It was not this room we walked to as we veered off into a smaller tunnel. After walking for what felt like a mile, we finally stopped at a thick wooden door. Goethe brought out a large brass key and thrust it into the lock. Inside the room was a table and on the table, a small box.

"This has been waiting here for you for eighteen years," Goethe said, indicating the box. "I was beginning to wonder if you were ever going to come back for it."

Milo walked towards the box. "My father left something for me here?"

"Not you." The dwarf nodded his head to me. "Her. Her mother left it."

I couldn't sleep. My mind was still whirring with everything I'd learned yesterday, which was precisely nothing. My questions hadn't been answered, but more questions had been thrown my way. Goethe knew nothing about the shift in energy, nor did he say much about the dragons. What he did tell me was that a box had been there since I was a newborn. When he told me my mother had left it, I thought he meant my birth mother, that maybe she was leaving some kind of clue for me to find her, but now, over twelve hours later, I knew that was ridiculous. Why would my birth mother leave me a clue to who she was in a mine? A mine to which humans rarely ventured? She wouldn't, and of course, she hadn't. The box had been brought here by the queen, just a day or two after the day she adopted me.

My parents celebrated my birthday on December 28th, which was the day they adopted me, but they thought I was a few days old by then, so my birthday was probably on the 24th or 25th. I had no real way of knowing. I pulled the box out from under my bed, where I'd stashed it the night before and opened it again, afraid that I'd imagined the whole thing.

There, just as it had been the night before, sat a stunningly beautiful ruby necklace. I'd never seen anything like it before, and even Milo, who had a mother who made jewelry, agreed that it was one of a kind. Hundreds of rubies set in gold. My mother had all the money in the world, and yet, I couldn't imagine why she would leave something so beautiful in the mines. I couldn't imagine her going to the mines at all, but I could hardly ask her why. She was still asleep.

All Goethe could tell me was that it was full of powerful magic, though he didn't know the extent of it. He'd been too wary of it to touch it, and so it had sat in the box, locked in the room for eighteen years. I held it up to my neck and glanced at myself in the mirror. It really was the most exquisite piece of jewelry, but I couldn't feel the power Goethe had said was in it. I clasped it around my neck, waiting for something magical to happen, but the room remained the same. I wondered if my own magic would be enhanced by it and if I would be able to do something more than call the dragons. But even with my concentration on full, I was not able to conjure so much as a teacup...or a teabag. Not even a tealeaf. I was beginning to suspect that maybe these magical beings were in on some kind of weird conspiracy to make me think I was powerfully magic when I wasn't. So I could summon dragons. Maybe that wasn't a difficult thing to do?

Unclasping the necklace, I placed it back in the box and ran my fingers over the intricate metalwork. This was a part of my history, but I didn't know what it represented.

It made me want to know more about my history. It seemed that everyone knew about my past but me. The natural person to ask would be my mother, but she was asleep. My father had flat out refused to tell me more than I already knew, and Dahlia was remaining tight-lipped on the subject. I couldn't shake the feeling that somehow my past was related to all that was going on. It couldn't be a coincidence that I arrived just after the worst part of history was over, nor that things happening to me now indicated that it was repeating itself. I'd never been magic before. So why now? Why when my mother was cursed, and the darkness was coming back?

I jumped out of bed and dressed quickly. My father had relaxed the rules about me being in my room, but he was on an emotional knife-edge, and there was no telling when he'd fall back into his foul mood. Thankfully, Vasuki had kept to his word, and the dragons had kept to themselves, although that was probably because my father hadn't attacked yet. I still had to figure out what to do with the competition and my wedding, but that didn't seem as important as finding out who I was.

Remy was the only one at the breakfast table when I got there. His mood was greatly improved from the previous day. I wondered if my father had let him sleep in his bed all night like he had done when he was a young child. Remy used to suffer from night terrors and would wake up screaming at all hours. My mother used to take him into bed with her, where he would sleep soundly. He gave me a joyful wave as I walked into the dining room.

"Hi, Aza,"

"Hello, Beautiful," I said, kissing his forehead and swiping a bit of toast from his plate.

"Ha oh,"

"Sorry, Remy, of course, I meant handsome. You are the most handsome."

He seemed satisfied by my answer and went back to tucking into his eggs.

I ate my breakfast more slowly, pondering who best to

ask about my history. No one in the castle, that was for sure. If my father got wind of what I was up to, he'd only be mad again. So who? It had to be someone who was around when I was small. Someone who remembered me being brought to the castle from the adoption agency.

There was no one I could think of. The only people I really knew were the people who worked in the castle and some of my parent's friends. They were a no-no too. I couldn't trust them not to tell my father.

"Ok, Aza?"

I looked up at Remy, who had the most worried expression on his face. He was mirroring my own expression.

"I'm fine Handsome. I'm trying to think of someone who knew me when I was little...when we were little." Remy was only eleven months younger than me. We grew up together, almost as twins.

"Olly Polly."

Remy clapped his hands as though he'd just done something really clever, and he had. He was a genius.

Olivie Polmer, or Olly Polly, as Remy called her, was Remy's governess when we were small. She was a sweet young thing with ringlets of bright red hair. Remy was always transfixed by her. She left when I was ten as she was pregnant and wanted to be a full-time mother. Just as Dahlia had been, she'd been in my parent's service when Remy was born. She was a secretary or something, but she became Remy's governess. She cried the day she left. She and Remy had a special bond, and even now, she visited a lot and bought presents for Remy's birthday. She was almost family, even though she'd not worked here for seven years.

"Do you want to go and visit her?"

Remy bounced up and down in his chair and clapped his hands violently. I had to stand up and hug him to calm him down. He had a tendency to over-excitement, and especially so when Olly Polly was involved.

After breakfast, I told my father I was taking Remy to Zhore. It wasn't a lie. Olivie lived there with her husband and four sons. I just declined to mention why I was going. My father was too preoccupied to ask why anyway. He was knee-deep in paperwork. Waving a hand in my direction, he murmured an okay.

"Just take a guard with you. I don't want you two going out alone."

I ran back upstairs to ask Milo if he wanted to join us, but when I got there, Jack announced that Milo had the day off.

I either had to find another guard to go with us and risk them telling my father where I'd been, or I could disobey my father's orders...again.

A quick look at Jack told me that the second option was the most preferable. I knew where Milo lived. I could go and see him first. Then technically, I'd have a guard with me. Yeah, I was stretching the truth, but it was for the greater good.

Remy was ready and waiting in the entrance hall, as giddy as a schoolgirl. I noted that he'd got changed for the occasion, wearing a bowtie. He'd been made to wear one once for some formal occasion or other, and Olivie had mentioned how suave he was with it on. He'd was six years old at the time and had to be told what suave meant. I'd never seen him look so pleased with himself. He wore that bowtie all the time, and even now, over a decade later, he still pulled it out when Olivie visited…or when we visited her.

"Looking very suave," I said, using the term he'd come to associate with the bowtie. He grinned from ear to ear, as pleased as punch with himself, even though he'd paired the bowtie with a sweater and shorts.

After sending him back to his room to change into long

pants, I took his hand and left the castle quickly before my father could put much thought into where we were going and stop us. Olivie was my only chance to find out who I was without father finding out. She hadn't worked for us for years, and I trusted her to keep a secret. She still kept the secret that it was I that accidentally broke my mother's favorite looking glass by kicking a ball at it when I was eight years old. She told my mother a gust of wind had knocked it over.

The walk to Zhore was long and uneventful, and yet, I couldn't shake the feeling that something was going to happen. The weather was dull, with gray clouds but, thankfully, no more snow. Looking up towards the Fire Mountains, I couldn't see the dragons. It wasn't them that I was worried about, though. No, it was something else, something I couldn't quite put my finger on. Maybe it was just the darkness that everyone was talking about. The shift in magical energy. Maybe it was nothing, and I was paranoid. Who knew?

Milo was surprised to see me when he opened the door. He was even more surprised to see Remy, but he invited us both in.

I told him quickly what we were doing, and so he decided to accompany us

Olivie lived in a quiet part of town, away from the hustle and bustle of the main streets. Her little cottage had a garden, and though the soil here was not exactly ripe for growing things, she'd made the most amazing space out front with pretty stones and cacti. All of it was under a layer of snow as we walked up the path.

The door flung open before we'd even had a chance to knock. A whirlwind of red curls launched herself at Remy, followed by four little red-headed tornados.

Remy hugged them all, carrying Olivie's youngest inside

with him. I didn't know why, but Remy never had to be told to unsquash around Olivie's children. He was delicate with them, and they loved him almost as much as he loved them.

Olivie brewed up some tea while the three of us played with her young children.

"To what do I owe the pleasure?" she asked, placing the tea tray on a table and ruffling Remy's hair.

He responded with a wide smile.

I picked up a cup of tea while I deliberated what to say. In the end, I decided to go with the truth. "I'm here about my adoption. I want to know where I came from."

Olivie's face drained of all color.

"You four," she shouted at her kids. "Go upstairs and play for a bit."

There was a chorus of oh, Moms, but eventually, with a little help from Olivie's husband, all four of them went upstairs, leaving just the four of us.

"I was never asked, specifically, not to tell you anything. I was asked not to tell anyone, but as it's you..."

"My mother is asleep, my father is up to his eyeballs in stress, and I've no one else to ask."

She lowered her eyes and nodded. "What is it you want to know?"

"Anything. Which adoption agency they used, where they picked me up from...anything."

"I don't know about the first. There is only one adoption agency in Zhore as far as I know, but it was never mentioned. You kind of just appeared one day. The king and queen acted like it had been planned for a long time, but they were flustered and unsure of what to do. Your grandmother helped out a lot, but I had the feeling she didn't know that this was about to happen either. It was like we all woke up one day, and there was this new baby...except..."

She'd basically told me the same thing as Dahlia. I appeared from nowhere. "Except what?"

"I was doing a night shift the night you came. Your parents didn't pick you up from an adoption agency. You were delivered to the castle."

This was new. Why would an adoption agency drop a baby off in the middle of the night?

"There's more," Olivie continued. "I watched a woman bring you to the castle door and knock. She spoke to your parents for quite some time on the doorstep. I remember thinking that you must be awfully cold. It was a mild winter that year, and you were wrapped up warmly, but it was still winter, and I could see you were very tiny."

"Did my parents know you saw them?"

She shook her head. "No. I never told them, and I don't think anyone saw me. It was about two am, and I was looking out of one of the kitchen windows. The carriage that brought you was parked close to it, but I could still see past it to your parents..."

She hesitated.

"There's something else isn't there? Something you've not told me."

She took a deep breath. "It's something I've never told anyone. Not even your parents."

"What?"

"There wasn't just one baby in that carriage. I heard another baby crying."

Another baby. I wasn't the only one. Somewhere out there, I had a twin.

Continue the adventure in Throne of Fury

AFTER THE HAPPILY EVER AFTER...

There is more to these stories. You want to know what happens next right? Fast forward eighteen years…

Pick up book one now

PREQUEL

SLEEPING BEAUTY
1. Queen of Dragons
2. Heiress of Embers
3. Throne of Fury
4. Goddess of Flames

LITTLE MERMAID
5. Queen of Mermaids
6. Heiress of the Sea
7. Throne of Change
8. Goddess of Water

RED RIDING HOOD
9. King of Wolves

10. Heir of the Curse
11. Throne of Night
12. God of Shifters

RAPUNZEL

13. King of Devotion
14. Heir of Thorns
15. Throne of Enchantment
16. God of Loyalty

RUMPELSTILTSKIN

17. Queen of Unicorns
18. Heiress of Gold
19. Throne of Sacrifice
20. Goddess of Loss

BEAUTY AND THE BEAST

21. King of Beasts
22. Heir of Beauty
23. Throne of Betrayal
24. God of Illusion

ALADDIN

25. Queen of the Sun
26. Heiress of Shadows
27. Throne of the Phoenix
28. Goddess of Fire

CINDERELLA

29. Queen of Song
30. Heiress of Melody
31. Throne of Symphony
32. Goddess of Harmony

ALICE IN WONDERLAND

   33. Queen of Clockwork

   34. Heiress of Delusion

   35. Throne of Cards

   36. Goddess of Hearts

WIZARD OF OZ

   37. King of Traitors

   38. Heir of Fugitives

   39. Throne of Emeralds

   40. God of Storms

SNOW WHITE

   41. Queen of Reflections

   42. Heiress of Mirrors

   43. Throne of Wands

   44. Goddess of Magic

PETER PAN

   45. Queen of Skies

   46. Heiress of Stars

   47. Throne of Feathers

   48. Goddess of Air

URBIS - Coming soon

   49. Kingdom of Royalty

   50. Kingdom of Power

   51. Kingdom of Fairytales

   52. Kingdom of Ever After

JOIN US

Would you like FREE Kingdom of Fairytales Coloring pages? Click the link below to pick your free gift up.
  Kingdom of Fairytales FREE gift

Check the Kingdom of Fairytales website for competitions, news and info on all the books and authors
  Kingdom of Fairytales Website

Or Join us on our Kingdom of Fairytales Facebook page for fun, games and author takeovers

Still want more? Completely immerse yourself in the Kingdom of Fairytales experience and pick up exclusive offers and gifts
  Become a Patron

A NOTE FROM THE AUTHOR

The Kingdom of Fairytales authors hope you enjoyed this new way of reading. We don't think that a series has ever been set with one chapter a day thought a whole year before and we hope we did it justice.

With this in mind, please leave a review, but when you do, remember that these books were always meant to be short breaks in your day and the blurb reflects that.

We would LOVE it if you can drop us a few words on Amazon

Review here

THE KINGDOM OF FAIRYTALE TEAM

These books would not be written without a great many people. Here is our team:

Many thanks to those who have made this possible.

Thank you to Rhi Parkes without whom, this series would never have come about.

Thanks to all the authors.

J.A. Armitage, Audrey Rich, B.Kristen Mcmichael, Emma Savant, Jennifer Ellision, Scarlett Kol, R. Castro, Margo Ryerkerk, Zara Quentin, Laura Greenwood and Anne Stryker

Also thank you to our amazing Beta team

Nadene Peterse-Vrijhof, Diane Major, Kalli Bunch and Stephanie Pittser.

ABOUT THE AUTHOR

J.A lives in a total fantasy world (because reality is boring right?) When she's not writing all the crazy fun in her head, she can be found eating cake, designing pretty pictures and hanging upside down from the tallest climbing frame in the local playground while her children look on in embarrassment. She's travelled the world working as everything from a banana picker in Australia to a Pantomime clown, has climbed to the top of Mount Kilimanjaro and the bottom of the Grand Canyon and once gave birth to a surrogate baby for a friend of hers.

She spends way too much time gossiping on facebook and if you want to be part of her Reading Army, where you'll get lots of freebies, exclusive sneak peeks and super secret sales, join up here

https://www.subscribepage.com/v7o8k4

Somehow she finds time to write.

Printed in Great Britain
by Amazon